About the Author

Anita Oswald (1976–Current) Anita was born in Groton, New London, CT, and currently still lives in New England, however she did most of her growing up in California. She holds a Bachelor's degree in English Language and Literature, and an associate degree in Marketing with a minor in Business Management. When Anita is not writing, she is mom to her daughter and adorable pup. Anita is a humanitarian/community volunteer at heart who loves to travel, a foodie, novice photographer, and lover of tequila and tacos.

Brother Where Art Thou

Anita Oswald

Brother Where Art Thou

Olympia Publishers
London

www.olympiapublishers.com
OLYMPIA PAPERBACK EDITION

A CIP catalogue record for this title is
available from the British Library.

ISBN: 978-1-80074-332-8

This is a work of fiction.
Names, characters, places and incidents originate from the writer's
imagination. Any resemblance to actual persons, living or dead, is
purely coincidental.

First Published in 2022

Olympia Publishers
Tallis House
2 Tallis Street
London
EC4Y 0AB

Printed in Great Britain

Dedication

If I end up in federal prison for my browser history, I'm blaming Lee. But seriously, this book belongs to all the local haunts I sat in for hours on end only to get two or three paragraphs written. The coffee made to perfection. The beer that helped get me through "that scene". The food which always distracted me way too much, and the people in my favorite spots who always just knew when I needed a refill and a break.

Acknowledgements

Thank you just doesn't seem like enough, when I add up all of the times I asked you to take Jasper out, because "I can't lose my groove". Or all the times I locked myself in a room with my laptop and texted you my Starbucks order before bribing you with a cake pop and frappuccino if you would go get it. Taylor, you are the absolute best of me, and hands down the best wing daughter a momma like me could ever have. I love you to the moon and back forever and always.

Prologue

"If I catch you saving food for later one more time…" She raised her fist high in the air, above her head, gripping the wooden paddle tightly, she let her hand drop, smacking the paddle against my exposed bottom with a loud *THWACK!* "This beating will pale in comparison to the next!" Without any second thought, my mother pushed me off of her lap to land in a sobbing heap on the floor at her feet. When she stood up, there was no mistaking the look of disgust on her face before she spit on me, her warm saliva landing on my cheek, and purposely letting the toe of each foot roughly connect with my stomach as she stepped over me.

As she reached the door, she turned around and said, "I suggest you get yourself cleaned up before your uncle gets home." And then slammed the door shut behind her, the sound of locks clicking into place just before her footsteps echoed off down the hall.

It's hard to say how long I lay there on the cold, rough, wooden floor next to my bed. Or what was supposed to be my bed, but was really more of a pallet with an old lumpy feather mattress on top of it. There was no pillow, and the one blanket I had was threadbare and dirty from years of use.

It hadn't always been like this, and I didn't always know what broken ribs felt like. For the past three years, if my tally of the days was correct, had been the worst of my life, and they didn't look to be getting any better. My stomach hurt so much from my jerking sobs, but more so from the kicks it had taken combined with hunger pains, not having eaten anything since last night. Apparently, the weaker I was, the easier it was for them to do what they did.

There were no windows in my little room, so it was hard to tell the time of day, and I couldn't hear any noises from outside, or inside for that matter. I suppose if I didn't want to suffer another beating, worse than the last, I should get up, and do as I'm supposed to. It hurt so much to move.

There was a toilet and sink in the corner of my room, no walls for privacy, although without any windows, did it matter? There wasn't even a bathtub or shower. My mother considered it a huge concession, and kindness on her part, to allow me a towel and cloth to wash myself with water from the sink. My private parts were always the worst to clean; they always hurt so much from my uncle's ministrations.

At first, when he started coming to my room, I cried, a lot, which made it worse. Something about me crying turned him on even more. As the days passed, I learned to hold my tears back, at least until I was alone in my nightmare, but this seemed to anger him, so he would hurt me more if I didn't cry. No matter what I did, I just couldn't... God, why couldn't they just let me suffer in silence?

After washing, I pulled my dirty oversized t-shirt over my head; it used to be my brother's. My mother made me wear it as part of my penance. When this one got too dirty and too smelly for her to bear it, she replaced it with another one, and another after that, it was never-ending.

When I crawled into my bed, I curled up on my side facing the wall, pulling my knees to my chest. I thought about how I ended up here. My mother claims it was because we were too close; it wasn't right. It was a sin. When he finally left in the middle of the night, because he couldn't take it any more, she punished me and said it was my fault, my doing; that if I didn't act like such a little slut, he never would have left her.

The sound of locks turning draws me from the dark recesses of my mind just before I smell my uncle's disgusting cologne, the stench of cigarettes clinging to his clothes, alcohol on his breath, and what I like to call au de horse breeding; a mixture of hay and manure soaked in foal after birth.

"My, my, my, look at that sweet little ass, all red from a beating." With the door now closed behind him, he walks over to my bed. His cold fingertips on the bare skin of my bottom make me flinch, he laughs and says, "Warm to the touch. Just like that sweet little pussy of yours."

I hear the zipper of his pants as he undoes them, and then the weight of his clothes landing on the floor.

His breath is warm on the nape of my neck as he reaches his hand around to roughly cup one tiny breast. "You know what to do, little girl."

And, I silently beg for God to just let me die already…

Chapter One
The Cave

"PLEASE, PLEASE NO! AAHHHHH, GOD" The sobs fuel my hunger, which makes me push harder, the hot poker eating into her skin, drawing more blood, *yes... more. I must have more.* "Please... I'll do anything, ju... just... oh God please, I'm begging you..." More sobs, more screams, more blood, more burning flesh. The shape of my signature looks perfect along the curve of her creamy, flesh-covered hip; one curve connecting to the other until it's finished. I always take my time with them, drawing the process out, letting my guest know that I care about them. Letting them know that I am focused solely on them.

This one passes out quickly, she's tiny, but I thought maybe she had more stamina than that. I'll have to show her how much this displeases me when she wakes up. Placing my poker on the metal tray next to me, I take a final look at my art before turning to walk over to the sink. Taking off my blood-stained gloves, I drape them over the side of the sink, and pull on a fresh pair before heading over to my command center.

On the center screen I check my guest's heart rate, weak but manageable. I will have to go slow with this one. For a few moments, my mind gets lost along with the sound of the soft beeps, and the slow rhythmic pattern of the lines on the screen. What must she be feeling right now? Is she numb from the pain? She doesn't know how truly special she is to have been chosen by me. I have such wonderful plans for her while she is here with me. A motion on the monitor to my left grabs my attention; it's only a bunny playing in the tall grass. After a more focused look around the grounds, it isn't a huge surprise that there isn't a single soul lurking around the area. Not that they would hear her screaming if they were, but rather sad that I won't have an audience today. No need to lament on that subject; there will be other opportunities.

On the screen to my right, I open an email from a friend. It's an invitation to a gathering in celebration of the Derby Festival, and my friend wants to know if I plan to make it; I respond, telling her that I will be there.

Derby Festival is one of my favorite times of year in Kentucky; there is so much fun to be had with all the parties, excitement with the race, and of course, meeting the people who all want a piece of the pie that is Derby Festival. When I was little, my parents used to take me with them on race day to the Downs; we would get to sit in the stands while they waited to see if their bets proved fruitful. Eventually though, they stopped taking me with them. At the time, it didn't make sense to me, obviously, I was too young to understand fully, but now… now I understand quite well.

Sitting back in my chair, I tip my head up to the grey limestone dome above me to think, this cavern was filled with thousands of gallons of water less than ten years ago. That's how long it has taken me to come this far, a complete setup to make the likes of David Parker Ray, green with envy. The twinkle of two chandelier lights suspended from the ceiling, exact duplicates of the ones my mother used to obsess over during dinnertime when I was growing up, enchanting me into whimsical ideas. I want the originals, however, they aren't exactly free for the taking at the moment anyway. Eventually.

Curving down the arched wall is a metal staircase leading from the entry to the cave floor, just behind me. To the left of the stairs is the vault where I keep all of my instruments and next to that a display case where I show off my souvenirs from our time together, to the right, a room for my guests to wait in until it's time for their session to begin. Spinning back around to focus on my current guest, she is strapped at her wrists and ankles to the corners of a custom-built stainless-steel table that pivots on one central point for my particular need at the time of use. At this very moment, she is upright as if on a billboard, head dropped forward, breasts perky with rosy little nipples, displayed in the most intimate of ways. Stringy brown hair caked with mud and sweat falls forward, obscuring what I might have been able to see of her face if it was shorter.

Getting up from my chair, I walk closer to the center of the cavern, stopping just before the four steps that lead up to a limestone platform I affectionately refer to as *"my stage"*. In the center of the platform is my guest, and next to her is a tray that holds a selection of tools I had planned to use today. Not among them would be a pair of stainless-steel sheers; however, I did include a razor-sharp straight edge blade.

Making my way up to the table, I unlock the brake and move the table into a position with her legs slightly above her head, *time to wake up sleeping beauty*. It takes a few seconds, but with the sudden rush of blood to her brain, she comes awake with a soft pain-filled moan. Reaching my gloved hand up to her forehead, I gently push her hair back from her face, and her eyes flutter open. She starts to smile until she realizes it isn't the gentle touch of a lover, but that of her host. Of course, she was hoping to be waking from a terrible nightmare. With now wide, terrified eyes, she starts to sob, begging me to stop. Begging me to please let her go. I shush her into only quiet sobs with a finger to her lips before I level the table, and quickly climb on top of it, on top of her.

Straddling her tiny waist, I lean down and place two soft kisses on her lips. They are soft and plump, trembling against mine, just the way I like them. Reaching back behind me, I find the warm pink folds of her pussy, separating them with my fingers; she screams and bucks beneath me. I laugh at her attempt to deter me from my prize, and push my fingers into her vaginal opening, the tissue around it stretching. She tries and continues to fail, as I weigh more than her, to get me off of her, fresh tears flood her eyes, I lean down and lick them from her cheeks, *mmm, they taste so good...* all of her flailing causes my fingers to move rougher than intended inside of her, the skin of her hymen breaking far sooner than I intended. For that, she will be punished.

Removing my hand from between her legs, I sit up and lick the sparse amount of blood from my fingers; she squeezes her eyes closed, sobbing and screaming. Reaching over to the table with my now clean hand, I grab the straight razor and look at her face until she opens her eyes.

It takes a few moments, but the morbid curiosity always gets the better of them. It's part of our genetic make-up, our innate curiosity to know what's going on during a period of silence or intermission. Her eyes open, she whispers the word *"please"* as if I have had a sudden change of heart. *So sorry baby, but letting you go is not an option.* Leaning forward again, I kiss her forehead at the same time that I grab a fist full of her hair, and proceed to make several semi-circular cuts around the crown of her head; she bucks underneath me the entire time I strip her of her dirty brown locks. I try to show her what is now mine, and she wants nothing to do with it. Squeezing her eyes shut tight, she weeps and begs for death, which won't come as soon as she is hoping it will. We still have plenty of time to enjoy each other's company.

Chapter Two
Shelby

"And how did you feel during the investigation?"

That's a good question. How did I feel? "I don't know." It's not the answer he wants. He wants me to say something along the lines of, "*I was devastated*", or "*I was so broken up over it that I couldn't function for weeks afterword.*" Fuck I can't stand this shit.

Dr Krane sits across from me with one leg crossed over the other at the knee, like some sort of pansy who can't bring himself to be anything less than perfect. He wears a brown tweed suit jacket with leather patches on the elbows, tan, perfectly pressed dress pants, and a white button-down shirt. To top off his perfect professor look, he has dainty wire-framed glasses, and a head of neatly combed brown hair. *Fuck! Why am I here again?*

The expression on Dr Krane's face says that he has all day to sit here and wait me out. In reality, we only have about fifteen minutes left of this session. *Thank fuck! I seriously need some bourbon.*

While I sit looking everywhere but at the good Dr, I admit to myself that I do know how I felt during the investigation of my mother's death; I felt free. I don't bother saying this out loud just yet. Part of me is afraid that when I do, all sorts of other feelings that I'm not ready for, are going to surface.

Another part of me is afraid that if I did say the words aloud, policemen would barge through the office door and lock me up for life.

We sit there for another five minutes, Dr Krane periodically taking notes, observations of my behavior, or lack thereof. I pass the time picking at my nails, or what's left of them, and focus on anything except the dark brown eyes that watch me with far too knowing a gaze.

Finally, mercifully, he says, "Our time for today is up. We will revisit this conversation next week. Until then, think about my question, and remember you are in a safe place here. There is nothing for you to fear by speaking the truth of your thoughts." I respond with a tight smile and jerky nod before standing to leave his office, the door swinging closed behind me. It's only once I'm out in the waiting room that every muscle in my face is able to relax. My lips fall apart slightly, allowing me to take in a shaky breath. Unlike the room on the other side of the door, this one is bright and cheery.

Plush, oversized beige furniture waits for weary, depressed, sad and angry people to fall into it. Dark green plants line the windowsills, thriving from the vitamin D streaming through the ceiling height windows. For a pop of color, Dr Krane hung large abstract works of art on the walls; turquoise, orange, red, yellow, blue, and on and on go the different colors. There are only six pieces in total, but they are enough to make you feel lighter. They are enough to make you lose yourself in one trying to figure out where the different swirls, and lines are going. Like a rainbow threw up after a night of binge drinking. I was getting a headache. While Dr Krane likes to make his patients feel warm while they wait, he prefers his personal space to be on the colder more clinical side. Perhaps this is what prompts us or rather others, to open up more freely. Whatever the reason, I don't like being in his space. I would rather not be in anyone else's space either

After putting my sunglasses on, I head for the elevator, push the "L" button and wait. I suppose I could take the stairs; it is, after all, only seven flights down. Just as I am about to abandon my post and head for the stairwell, a ding sounds signaling the arrival of my chariot. I step in and do a double-take, my heart skipping several beats before kicking into high gear. I am positive that if I can hear it whooshing in my ears, then she can too. Thankful she can't see my huge bugged-out eyes, since I am still wearing my dark sunglasses, and that I have aged about nine years since we last saw each other, I pull myself together and will my legs to move. Trying to act nonchalant, I step into the opposite corner as her, angling my body in such a way that my face isn't open for examination.

If she has noticed my seemingly crazy antics, she doesn't let on. It is a huge relief, one that I am ready to celebrate until she says, "Did you really think I wouldn't recognize you, Ms Barnett-Bowman?" She draws out the "Ms" As if it is spelled with a thousand little "z's" after the "M." I am immediately transported back to the night we first met. It was a beautiful summer's evening, the sky dark, tons of flickering little fireflies scattered in the black void. It reminded me of when I was younger, and my brother and I would pretend they were trying to tell us something. We would flick our flashlight back at them, communicating sacred secrets we joked. Just as she had pulled me out of my thoughts then, she does so now with an overtly, and extremely annoying, clearing of her throat. "Of course I knew you would, Detective Gaines. She looks older, but not quite as old as she should. Or maybe she does, fuck I

22

don't know and I don't know why I'm even thinking about this, it doesn't matter. How are things?"

"Things," she says, emphasis on the word "things," "are just fine, thank you. How are things for you these days?"

Well, two could play that game. "Things are going well if not extremely busy," I say, and pray that the elevator hits the lobby before she can ask anything else. No such luck.

"Right. You took over the family business." It's no sacred secret, being the sole heir to my father's, and then uncle's wills, I now run the daily operations of Bowman Farm.

"That's correct. Someone has to do it." I say, lifting my chin into the air the smallest of measures. Defiantly daring her to say something about that night while I belatedly wonder what she is doing here, in this building, coincidentally on the same day and same time as me. Is she poking around in my past? Asking Dr Krane for information from our sessions? Can she even do that? No, doctor patient confidentiality is a thing. I need to stop being so paranoid.

Mercifully, the ding that signals we have reached the lobby level sounds, the doors slide open, and I start to make my way out of the elevator when she says, "You know, there's still one question I have from that night that I just can't seem to get rid of."

Logically, I know she is baiting me, but my curiosity gets the better of me. I want to know what she could possibly still have to ask after nine years, so I say, "And what's that?"

"Why would someone take pain killers, this specific one, knowing that they are allergic to them?"

"She was sick. She was confused. The lead investigator at the time ruled it an accident." An accident. Maybe if I keep

23

repeating it, an accident... an accident... It would make it true.

"Well, I suppose the only person who can answer the question" she pauses for a moment and then continues, "Is no longer able to." As if I need a reminder that my mother is dead. Buried six feet underground. Gone from this world and never to return.

I look at the woman standing in front of me, examining the little lines that now frame her lips and eyes before I give her a tight-lipped smile and say, "Thank you for the reminder." Turning, I walk briskly out of the building, not paying attention to where I am going exactly, but wanting to get away from the unwanted reminders of my past and dive face-first into a vat of bourbon.

It doesn't take me long to find a bar. In fact, I pass several of them before choosing this one. It's a dive if ever I had seen one. A virtual hole in the wall, the interior is dark, the only light coming from a few dingy light bulbs inside even dingier glass globes. It smells of stale cigarettes, cheap booze, and body odor. I'm about to sit on an empty stool at the bar, and think better of it before making my way to an empty booth in the barely lit back corner. I have sorrows to wallow away in, and I don't want some nosey bartender watching and judging. Trying to be my second therapist of the day.

What is with that anyway? Not that I care what some sleazeball barkeep thinks, but I do want to maintain some modicum of decorum. I ask for a bottle of the best bourbon he has, which not to my surprise, is way off the mark, and a shot glass. I can still be civilized with my self-destructive behaviors.

The first one goes down hard; the cheaper the bourbon, the worse the burn. The second and third go much smoother as

I decide to pace myself, and take my time with number four. I remember all of the times I watched my dad sip Bourbon at his desk while he worked, he liked to savor it and let the flavors coat his tongue, rolling the liquid of his first sip around once, twice, then a third time before swallowing. I never understood why he did this until I started drinking bourbon myself. It stings the mouth; it sets a small fire on your tongue, and leaves a lingering but healing heat in its wake. This shit just straight up burns. I imagine it feels, and tastes like, what a gallon of turpentine would feel and taste like if you swallowed that.

Just as I'm finishing off number five, my cell buzzes in my pocket with a reminder that I have a meeting with a prospective client in exactly thirty minutes. It's going to take me forty minutes to get back to the farm.

The farm. The place where it all began and the place where it will likely all end; for me anyhow. The family business. But is it still a family business if you're the only one in the family still living? I suppose it is. It's a legacy after all. Champions have been born there, studded there, and even died there.

Chapter Three
Harper

I absolutely love this place. It isn't the typical stuck-up fru-fru martini bars that the girls like to frequent on our nights out. You know, the ones that have tiny little velvet stools, around even tinier, polished silver, round tables. They serve drinks that have weird names like; *"The Blacksmiths Daughter"* or *"Purple Rain Clouds"*, and cost almost as much as my newest Burkin bag. Black lacquered floors you can see yourself in that are waxed to perfection. When you walk, you could almost break an ankle from slipping on them in seven-inch stilettos. But this place is all jeans and t-shirts, flip flops, country music, wide-open doors, and not an overly sweet drink on the menu. In fact, there are only six drinks to choose from, and they are all beers brewed right here in this very building.

Usually, I don't pay much attention to the people around me, those outside of my immediate circle, that is, but here... here it's hard not to take in the humans that I'm sharing such a quaint, intimate space with. While I sip my Emma Wood; fruity, wheat summer ale, I watch the bartender chat up some regulars at the opposite end of the white pine slab of wood, and wonder what it would be like to be so casual, so informal, so cool. I suppose I am pretty cool, as far as my friends are concerned. It's a daily struggle to try and do anything that isn't immediately copied by everyone in my social circle, or more accurately, anyone within a three-hundred-mile radius on a bad day. With the Derby Festival coming into full swing, it's bound to get worse, which is why I find myself here, in this local, fifty-five miles from Louisville, microbrewery.

Last night while I was at dinner with my parents, it was all "Derby Festival this," and "Derby Festival that." My head almost exploded with the list of company and family obligations being rattled off by my mom and dad, not to mention the personal obligations I have. It was one thing to be the daughter of Lincoln and Ella Ward Lewis-Sheridan. Still, something else entirely to be Sheridan Reserves Chief Environmental Affairs Officer, never mind just being Harper Adalynn Ward Lewis-Sheridan. It's a mouthful, I know! My mother has expectations, the company has expectations, my dad has expectations as both my boss and my dad, and my friends have expectations too. I was expectationed out, and this is my way of spending at least three hours without any expectations being placed on my shoulders. It feels wonderfully magnificent.

I spin around on my squeaky bar stool, take another cursory glance around the roughly twelve hundred square foot room; my eyes stop on a pair of bright blues peering at me from just outside the raised garage-style door. Not a familiar face, but a handsome one, that's for sure. I spin back around just in time to watch two of the bartenders, who I earlier learned are the owners, take a picture with a cute blonde in a white dress and jean jacket, all three, wearing red, plastic fire hats. Through a little conversation with Jim, the third bartender, I learn that she works here, and has just graduated from fire fighter's academy. I don't know that I have ever seen a woman firefighter before, and she's so… not just cute, but

27

pretty. Very pretty. And brave. I imagine it takes something strong inside of a person to want to run into a burning building to save a complete strangers life. Good for her.

Sitting here among all of the people who seem so close and familiar with one another, I feel like an interloper. A stranger crashing a family reunion, and I don't feel bad about it at all. I like it. I like how the vibe in this place courses through me, fills every crevice of my being with spirit, fun, and something else. Something I can't quite put my finger on. "Another Victory?" The bartender asks. He isn't speaking to me, though; he's asking the guy who just stepped up next to me.

"That, and one of whatever the lovely lady is having."

I swallow the last sip of my beer and look up into the same brilliant blue eyes from earlier. He is much better looking than I initially thought. Dark brown hair, arranged in a haphazard way, a hint of two-day-old morning shadow covering his jaw and chin.

He's wearing a dark blue quarter-zip and jeans. "Thank you," I say a little too brightly. Maybe I should decline and head home. But those eyes... They are drawing me in and make me feel like it's a warm summer's day in the pool, a margarita in one hand, and nothing but time to pass while lazily floating from end to end, and back again.

"It's my pleasure." He holds his hand out and says, "Matt."

Taking his hand in mine, I say, "Harper. It's nice to meet you."

"Harper. That's a pretty name, but I'm sure you've heard that before."

"I have. So why don't you tell me something that I don't

already know." *Holy shit!* Whatever they put in the Emma Wood is making my tongue looser than fuck, or I've had one too many. It's probably the latter.

He laughs a hearty chuckle before saying, "You and I are going to fuck against the wall in the bathroom."

Jim laughs and shakes his head, clearly knowing this man's antics well. So I feign disgust before laughing so hard that I fall forward, my forehead lands on my arm. When I look up, Matt isn't laughing. In fact, he has a seriously cocky smile on his face. I sober immediately, but my tingling lady bits remind me that I haven't had sex in weeks, and I need a release. "Okay." The one word slips out of my mouth before I can think better of it.

He laughs and says, "Why don't you come join my friends and me outside?"

I give him a saucy smile, emboldened by Emma, and say, "Lead the way."

Adventure. That's what else this place makes me feel, a sense of adventure.

Matt's friends are hysterical and so welcoming. Spending time with them makes me feel more alive than I have felt in a long time. They are animated, loud, vulgar, and so free with their thoughts. I find myself absorbing their energy and storing it away for use later. There will definitely come a time in the next couple of weeks when I will need to tap into it for self-preservation purposes. I find myself laughing so much that my face hurts, talking so loudly that my throat will have that raw feeling tomorrow morning, and before I can think too much about tomorrow morning, Matt, who has just lost at Jenga, comes over to stand behind me. He places one hand on the curve of my hip; he is so close I can feel all of the hard plains of his body against my back.

Leaning in, he whispers in my ear, "What do you say we get out of here?"

What do I say? I don't know this man. Do I play it safe and decline with the excuse of a long drive home? Do I take the risk and accept only to find myself in the secret lair of a serial killer? *HURRY UP AND DECIDE, YOU LOONY...* "Okay." Matt does a bang-up job at hiding his momentary surprise at my acquiescence to his proposal.

Clearly, he thought the "good girl" in me was going to win out against his attempt to seduce my inner risk-taker. And ten minutes later, I find myself walking up a set of rickety stairs on the side of an apartment building headed for the third floor.

"Are you sure about this?" It's very kind of him to ask, but not necessary. "Because once you go through this door, all gentlemanly behavior is gone. I plan to ravage that body of yours in ways that will make you blush for weeks to come."

"I look forward to it," is all I can say before taking the leap and stepping over the threshold into his apartment.

"Get undressed."

Okay... He is just standing there. Leaning against the now-closed door to his home, watching me. I don't want to just strip down, too anxious and nervous like. So I stand here for a minute, watching him watch me. In my periphery, and in the dim light from the table lamp in the corner, I can see that he likes a clean modern style. Sleek black furniture with the shine of glass and chrome accents. Emboldened by having had more Emma Wood than I should have, I crouch down, slow and steady, to unzip my black leather Louboutin booties before kicking them off. His rug is so incredibly soft and plush under my feet, through my thin socks.

I'm standing upright again and channeling my inner

stripper. I'm going to make this man's mouth water for a piece of me. Slowly I move my hands to the waist of my jeans, popping one button, then another, followed by the slow descent of my zipper; the sound from it louder than it should be in the quiet room. Matt's eyes practically glow when he sees a little peek of the lace covering the apex between my thighs. But I'm not done. Next, I pull the bottom of my silk blouse out of my pants; it covers up anything he may have been able to see. Did he just growl at me?

I turn around slowly in a half-circle and begin to shimmy out of my skintight jeans. I make sure to bend over straight-legged, allowing him to get a nice view of my naked ass while I pull my jeans over my feet, taking my socks with them. I didn't notice it until I turned back around, but he had taken a few steps closer to me, eager to touch. To keep the anticipation up, I methodically start unbuttoning my shirt, one after the other, at a measured pace. I let it slip down my arms and fall to the floor behind me. I now stand in front of this man in only my peek-a-boo lace bra and panties.

His hunger for me is palpable, electric in the space that separates us. Reaching behind my back, I unhook my bra and hold it against my breasts for the briefest of moments before I dangle it from one hand then drop it to the floor. My panties are wet. I can feel the moisture pooling between my thighs. The ache in my pussy is intense. I just want him to touch me already, but he doesn't. Instead, he stands an arm's length away, looking me up and down before meeting my eyes, a questioning smile on his face. My panties... Right. I'm afraid that if I go anywhere near my pussy right now, I might explode; combust into a million pieces with any friction in that area. But I do it. I run my flattened palms over my hips and down my lower belly. My fingertips slip under the thin band of my thong, and hooking it under my thumb; I pull them down over my thighs. They fall to the ground. *What now?*

My brain is in overdrive. I'm feeling braver than I really am when I step up to Matt. I get all in his space and look up into his steamy gaze, except he is one step ahead of me and lifts me up off the ground, pins me against the closest wall, and buries his face in my pussy. It is by far the most blessed gift I could have received at this moment.

Tongue swirling, dipping in and out, he knows exactly where to go to bring me to release, not once, not twice, but three magically mind-blowing times, and he clearly isn't done with me, but then I'm not done with him either.

It's not until the next morning on my drive back to reality that I realize I left my panties on his living room floor. When I woke up this morning, it was to Matt lying next to me; he was watching me sleep. It was kind of cute. I tried to play it cool and slink out of bed, but he wasn't having that. We fucked two more times, a handful of orgasms later, we were in the shower, my back against the cool, wet glass wall, hot steam surrounding us while he made brunch out of my pussy, again. To be fair, I did the same for him before he fucked me into next week from behind, from the side, from every possible angle. It was amazing and then some. Once I could walk again, and after he made me breakfast, I made my way to Betty, my blacked-out Bugatti Veyron Grand Sport in a pair of his plaid boxers and one of his grey t-shirts. My clothes were piled on the passenger seat next to me, and a promise to come back and visit soon was left in the dust from my speedy exit onto the main road out of town.

Chapter Four
Nathan

Hot steamy water streams from the giant square showerhead above and flows like silk down the contours and curves of my body. It's hotter than it needs to be, but that's a necessary evil to wash away the sins of my night. Although it was fun while it was happening, I got quite tired of her incessant, nasally laughter every time I said something, even if it wasn't remotely funny.

Women like her are a dime a dozen, pretty, rich, and dumb. They bat their fake eyelashes at any sign of a compliment and spread their legs faster than God could part the Red Sea when they think you have more money than their daddy. The downside; they don't want to leave. They think that you're going to make them an honest woman. Sweep them off their feet, marry them, give them babies, and make their daddy proud of them for carrying on the line. And fortune. I'm not fool enough to get caught in that trap besides, I didn't leave this life to get sucked back into it by some unemployed debutant whose sole focus in life is to catch the fattest payday in the pond. Unfortunately, I need this one, so my customary walk to the door before dawn didn't happen today.

Sleeping beauty is still oblivious to the world waking around her when I emerge from my walk-in closet dressed and prepared for the day ahead. One last tug to adjust my tie before

I sit next to her naked body, barely covered by the silk of the black sheets on my bed; I run the tip of pinkie across her forehead. This does the trick and she stirs with a soft moan, I'm guessing from comfort, "Time for me to leave."

"Mmmm…" In her sleepy voice she says, "Come back to bed."

"Sorry, but business calls. Let's have dinner?"

"Okay. What time?"

"I'll get back to you on that." I stand up and continue, "I have to check my schedule with Amy and…"

"Who's Amy?"

I don't even try to hold back my laugh, saying, "She is my executive assistant."

"I see. Well, when you figure out what time you are free; text me." It's all nonchalance and poorly hidden jealousy.

It isn't my style to soothe such wounds, however in this case I walk back over to the bedside and place a light kiss on her lips, "Rest assured, it will be the first thing I do upon my arrival at the office." It doesn't take much sometimes.

Closing the door behind me, I swiftly walk down the hallway past several closed double doors, each leading to one of three guest bedrooms, a guest bathroom, and at the end, before the stairs, a home gym. The main staircase in this place was listed as one of the most prominent features when I bought it just about a month ago. Virtually invisible, not only are they the floating kind, but clear and light up at night. Not really my style, but then that's not why I bought the place. The already existing and easily upgradeable state-of-the-art security system, panic room, and dead space in the floor are. I have a feeling those are going to come in handy over the next…

"Good morning Mr Barnett. Do you want the car brought

around?"

"Yes, please. And good morning, Lee." I take the cup of coffee he hands me and say, "Thank you for making sure the house set up went smoothly." Per his usual response, I get a slightly cockeyed nod of the head before he walks back into the kitchen. He is a gruff sort of guy with a wicked sense of humor, loyal, and his cooking is off the charts. "Lee..." I follow him into the kitchen, "Could you make sure that Ivy..." I point up at the ceiling for reference, "is up and out of the house before lunch, please? We don't need her overstaying her welcome." Another knowing nod, but this time followed with a chuckle.

Outside, Tom, who is one hell of a handyman but also happens to be Lee's husband, hops out from behind the wheel of my Storm Noir Bentley Continental GT V8, "She's all tuned up and drives like a dream."

"Thanks, Tom." I move to get into the driver's seat, but remember... "When Ivy, my guest from last night, leaves, I know how much you hate doing it, but could you please use the Mulsanne to drive her home?"

Through his groan of discontent, he agrees, and stomps off like a petulant child dismissing my laugh and thanks.

"Good morning Mr Barnett." Amy, my executive assistant, is sitting behind her desk when I walk into the office. Today her hair is platinum blonde and grey-ish; it's an ever-evolving process.

"Good morning, Amy. Love the hair." She doesn't flatter easily. When I first hired Amy seven years ago, she was working part-time days as a cashier at the local mall and nights as a call girl, albeit high-end, but still a call girl. She had shown up at my hotel room in Austin, TX, by mistake. It was the man next door who had "ordered" her, but by the time the evening was over, we had, had dinner, laughed, and found that we liked each other's company as much as an older brother likes that of his younger sister. Three days later I was in need of an assistant, and she agreed to take on the task. All these years later we still work like a well-oiled machine just out of the factory.

Per usual, all of the files that need to be reviewed today are stacked neatly next to the list of calls I need to return, and mail I need to sort through. And that's after Amy does a first pass through, it seems that even when temporarily away from my home office in Seattle, the requests for donations, interviews, and appearances still flood the inboxes. "Amy, before I forget, what does my schedule for tonight look like?"

Walking through the open double French doors that separate our offices, she says, "You have drinks with Lincoln Ward-Sheridan at six, a conference call with Lee Shen at seven our time, and then you're free."

"Could you move drinks with Sheridan to tomorrow night? And I need you to call the house and ask Ivy, my guest, if an early dinner at five-thirty would work for her?"

"A female overnight guest? That's new."

"Yes, well… Please, Amy?" I give her a look that says, *"don't ask anything more."*

"Sure." Laughing softly, she walks back to her desk, and does as I asked. It only takes her a few minutes to return and confirm that the calls were made, and my calendar is now updated. Of course, she throws in that Ivy sounds like a total dingbat before getting back to work. That's one way to describe her.

The words "*you need her*" play on an endless loop in the back of my mind all morning and afternoon while I work. She, fortunately for me, has an in with a certain person I'm planning to "bump" into. I could use the fact that I'm the silent benefactor for her family's business; the one that flooded money into it after her uncle died and her mom and the foreman, selected by her uncle to run the business until she turned twenty-one, nearly ran it into the ground. But I'm not going to. I would rather save that tidbit of info for use another day. Of course, I could also tell her...

"Nathan Barnett's office." I hear Amy say with her usual silvery tone followed by her perfected matter-of-fact response. She continues to say, "I'm sorry, but Mr Barnett is unavailable at the moment. May I take a message?" This piques my interest; it's not often that Amy screens my calls in this manner. This tells me it's either a tabloid looking for information or my adopted sister looking for money. My bet is on the latter.

"Uh huh... okay... right. Got it. I will tell him you called. Goodbye."

"My sister?"

"How'd you know?"

"That disgusted undertone to your voice whenever she calls."

"She's such a leach... Uhg... Why you continue to support her stupidity is beyond me."

"You're right. It is beyond you." I say with a friendly but warning smile.

"Sorry. She just..."

"I know." Returning to my desk, I dig into my files and put the thought of my adopted sister out of mind. The last time

37

she called, it was to ask for two hundred and fifty thousand to invest in some pyramid get-rich-quick scheme. I gave her half that and she lost it at the track betting on horses, booze, and cheap women within a couple of days. And yet, people still wonder why I don't bring her into the fold of Barnett Enterprises. The Seattle Times once called me ruthless and cold because of my desire to leave Kendra in the wings. It's not like our adopted status is legal in any official capacity, so there is that.

Five thirty comes all too quickly as I find myself relinquishing my car to the valet at Vincenzo's, an upscale Italian eatery with enough exclusivity and notoriety to make Ivy salivate for more. Of course, she is already there and seated in a tan velvety, circular booth. She looks pretty. Her hair is up in a pin-straight high ponytail. Her dress is tight... But then, I didn't expect anything less. Her goal is to end up in my bed for the second night in a row; she is going to be disappointed for sure.

We have made it halfway through our main course, or shall I say that I have blessedly survived to this point, when Ivy practically swallows her tongue while staring over my right shoulder. I turn my head and see the most gorgeous creature walking towards us. Her strawberry blonde hair shimmers under the low lighting in the dining room, creamy porcelain skin as elegant as silk covers every exposed inch of her, and those vibrant green eyes are accented by light makeup, giving her a polished to perfection look. She is wearing short white and black pinstriped shorts, a black silk blouse tucked into the shorts, and a matching pinstriped suit jacket. The look is finished with black heels at the end of her slender, mile-long legs. I have to catch myself and remember my place when I hear Ivy clear her throat from her near choking.

"Hello, Ivy. What a surprise seeing you here tonight. How have you been?" Her slow yet polished southern drawl is beautiful in its cadence. She finally meets my gaze, extends her hand, and says, "I don't think we have previously made each other's acquaintance."

Standing as most polite gentlemen do, I start to introduce myself when Ivy says, "Harper, it's so nice to see you as well. Things have been so incredibly busy, what with my Derby party coming up and all."

Completely ignoring Ivy, I grasp Harper's hand and am met with a firm handshake. "Nathan Barnett."

"How nice to meet one of Ivy's?" Looking between the two of us, she fills in with, "Friends." Her smile is like the warm sun after a chilly rain shower. "I'm Harper Lewis-Sheridan. It's a pleasure to meet you, Mr Barnett." Fuck my life.

"What brings you here tonight, Harper?"

Answering Ivy's question, she says, "Dinner with a few business associates." That smile ... she's trying to make a devil out of me. "I'm glad I was able to bump into you though, I've been meaning to respond to your email."

"Oh?"

"I'll be attending with a few friends if that's all right with you?"

"Of course. The more, the merrier."

"Perfect! It really is nice to see you Ivy, and to meet you, Mr..."

"Nathan. Please. Call me Nathan."

"Nathan. Enjoy your dinner." She says before walking off

to one of the restaurant's private dining rooms, where the patiently-waiting hostess opens the double French doors for her entry. This also affords me a glimpse into the room where the Kentucky State Senator, Governor, and their respective wives await if I'm not mistaken.

"Well, that was… perfect!" Ivy is positively radiating with her excitement. "I'm sorry?" Clearly, I've missed something here.

"I heard she might be having dinner here tonight, so it was the perfect opportunity to kill two birds with one stone."

"And which two birds would those be?"

"Oh, you know; showing off my sexy new man, and also getting a confirmation from *THE* Harper Ward-Sheridan about my Derby party. Of course, she is bringing her entourage, LKB, as she always does. Silly me, that's Lucy, Kendal or Kenny, and Bryan, so you know. It's perfect really, I expected as much, but this will bring so many more paparazzi to my front door. I should call the caterer and tell her we need to step up the menu…" And on and on and on she went. I tuned out after Champagne tower, completely consumed by my own thoughts and Harper Ward-Sheridan.

"And what do you think about maybe doing a fun, kitschy photo booth out in a little tea garden like area?"

Midway through rethinking my strategy with Lincoln Ward-Sheridan, Ivy clears her throat in a clear *excuse me* manner. I'm a natural multitasker, "I'm sure it will go over well. Insta worthy for sure." She lets off a squeal like a new piglet waiting to suckle a teat for the first time, which prompts me to look at my Jaeger-LeCoultre watch. After mentioning that I have to get back to the office for an international conference call, she pouts. I cringe. We make our way out of the restaurant, and she practically begs me to come over after my call. I promise nothing and leave her hanging, but not before giving her a sultry kiss and playful smack on her ass with plenty of witnesses around to see it; reminders to myself that I still need her.

Chapter Five
Shelby

Oddly I find comfort in the smell of the stables. Each has its own variation of a horse, hay, and fertilizer stench, but this particular one makes me want to puke every time I step foot in it. This is the stable where, when I was only two years old, I found my father face down in a pile of dirty hay. After only twenty-four hours, the police ruled his death the result of a major heart attack and closed the case. Subsequently, this left my uncle as the new figurehead for Bowman Farm until his death ten years later.

Coincidentally, it happened in this same stable.

Sadly, this was my father's favorite stable, which is why he was out here the night he died. Although I was only two at the time, I can still remember that night pretty vividly. My Mother and Brother were only a few steps behind me; I waddled into the stable through a slightly open door, giggling and chattering in toddler nonsense. That's when I saw my daddy lying there on the ground. At first, in my naive child's mind, I thought he was playing a game with me, so I climbed on his back, pretending to ride him like a horse. This is something we did often; he would crawl around the large rooms of our home on his hands and knees while I sat on his back. We would pretend we were racing in the Derby, coming in second place until the last second on the clock when we pulled ahead and won by the skin of our teeth. This wasn't the case that night. That night there was no celebration in the winner's circle surrounded by my mother and brother.

That night they surrounded me for a very different reason. My Mother had pushed me off my daddy's back, screaming and crying hysterically while my brother held me apart from them as farmhands poured into the stable to help. Soon after that, sirens sounded loud, piercing my ears, blue and red lights spinning on the walls around us like a kaleidoscope of nightmares. It was the night that forever changed my life.

"I knew I would find you in here."

Harper's soft feminine voice pulled me from my past while I remained standing there with my back to her. I knew she would show up at some point. She always did on this day. It's funny, actually; we were never friends before I found out about our shared past. Don't get me wrong, we weren't enemies either, we were just acquaintances who lived in the same town since birth, frequented the same locations, and mingled in the same circles. We both came from affluent families who practically built and owned this town.

After my mother died, I spent several months going through her things; papers, journals, material belongings, and a safety deposit box in an effort to purge the bitch from my life forever. In that safety deposit box, I found documents and news clippings that pertained to my birth, and to Harper's birth. Given that we are from two very different families with zero relation to one another, I expected her to have documents about my birth but thought it was odd, and a bit startling, that she had medical documents regarding a second female baby delivered on the same day as me, one minute after me, and from the same womb as me. Along with those documents, there were news clippings to announce my birth and the birth of another baby girl to another family on the same day. The Lewis-Sheridan family had named their daughter Harper while I was named Shelby.

At first, I thought maybe my parents didn't want two babies, so they gave the second up for adoption, which made me so angry given what happened to me after my father died. I then quickly moved past that thought and remembered how different Harper and I looked from one another. It confused the fuck out of me for so long. Twins don't always look alike; I mean, there had to be a logical reason for this. Right? I held onto what I thought I knew for about a year before I approached Harper with it. Jesus, was she ever mad at me. We weren't even friends, and there I was, claiming that she was my long-lost twin sister. After yelling at each other, crying, and slinging all sorts of insults back and forth, she grabbed my arm, hauled me off to her father's office, and demanded that he explain what the *"ever-loving fuck"* was going on. Her words, not mine. I thought her dad was going to smack her a good one, but when he saw me next to her, he came over to us, scooped us both up into a huge hug, and cried. We were both stunned, motionless. Once he got that out of his system, he called her mom, telling her to meet us at the place.

Turns out, *"the place"* was an empty field at the bottom of a limestone cliff wall that extended at least four hundred feet upward. At the base of the rock wall, there was an opening to a cave, with a danger sign prohibiting entrance. Across from that, there was an abandoned hydroelectric plant built on a lock and dam extending across the rushing river once used to power homes in the area, and an old abandoned shack a few feet away from the bank of the river.

Harper's Mom was already there when we arrived; she stood under a huge oak tree, basking in the cool shade as relief from the humid temperatures of the mid-day sun. Her blonde hair was up in a sleek chignon, she had on a teal-colored sheath dress, and nude-colored pumps lay haphazardly on the ground next to her. Her back was to us while her husband navigated his car into the clearing next to hers. Her arms were wrapped around her torso, her head bent slightly downward. Harper lightly noted out loud that her mom was standing barefoot in the dirt and grass. Her statement weighed heavily on both of us, until the gravity of our situation was thrust upon us with the news that we were, in fact, born from the same womb.

It wasn't, however, as I initially thought. Harper and I were not long-lost sisters. We were born as the result of a phenomenon called superfecundation. Apparently, this phenomenon happens when two different fathers fertilize two eggs released during the same cycle at separate times. In our case, it was my father's sperm through sexual intercourse and Harper's Dad's sperm through in-vitro. Her parents couldn't conceive naturally, so my mother volunteered to be their surrogate in this supposed anonymous situation through happenstance. But my mother being the cunning bitch I then knew her to be, had figured out who the other party was and gathered her information to use for future blackmail, I assume. Since we were birthed in my parent's private residence with only one doctor and one nurse in the room, there wasn't any suspicion from my father or anyone else when they left, and one baby remained. I guess besides the doc and nurse, only my mother and the two people standing before us knew. *The Place* was where the nurse and doctor met Harper's parents to deliver them their new baby girl.

After that day, Harper never looked at me, or even acknowledged my existence for a long while, at least. She showed up here at the farm one day, finding me in the same spot on the same day in history, and from then on, we have been friends. Not the kind of friends that do everything together, but more like sisterly friends. We comfort each other when we need it, we fight like sisters often do, and we defend one another when a situation calls for it. We spend holidays together and even claim to be cousins when people ask why we are so close, like families often are.

"Where else would I be?"

Coming to stand next to me, we both gaze out of the open stable doors into the sprawling pasture beyond. In her hand, she is holding a bottle of Sheridan Reserve Baccarat by the long sleek neck. Named after the card game our fathers both coincidentally like to play together. It was her dad's tribute to my late father. It was also my father's favorite private reserve. At the time they played together, it was only made in small batches for Harper's Dads' private use and was unnamed. Sadly, it got its name shortly after my dad's death. The handcrafted crystal bottle full of amber liquid sells at about three thousand a bottle.

"Well, I thought maybe you would be about two feet to the left, you know, in the shade." She says it with a small smile. Her attempt to lighten the mood and it works.

With a snorted laugh, I step to the side into the shade, saying, "Right. I forgot you have that aversion to sun." Referring to her creamy smooth pale skin. Reaching out, "Hand it over," I was referencing the bottle in her hand.

"Wasting no time, I see." She somehow produces two rocks glasses, "We can at least be civilized drinkers."

With a loud *POP,* I pull the cork out of the opening and pour a double into each glass. The scent of spiced oak and fruit fills my nostrils. And before I have a chance to swallow my first dose down, Harper makes her usual toast.

"To the man from whom you descend, may he forever rest in peace; Happy birthday, Russell."

"Happy birthday, Daddy." We clink glasses and tip them back, both of us finishing in one smooth swallow.

"Did you respond to Ivy's email invite?"

"Uhg… Yes, only because you wouldn't stop pestering me about it. You know I can't stand her."

"I know, but it will be good for you to get out of the house for something other than work-related stuff."

"I'm going to your parents' party!"

"That doesn't count." She says it very matter-of-factly, as if it makes one bit of difference to me. A party is a party.

"How do you figure?"

"At my parents' party, it will be a bunch of industry goons trying to kiss my daddy's ass, their wives all drooling over this and that, and stuffy celebs who just want a paparazzi picture to prove that they were there." I give her that "*and your point is*" look as she continues to say, "At Ivy's, you will get to hang out with moi, and…"

I cut her off and say, "I can do that at your parents' party too."

"But you won't get to meet Ivy's new man candy." She says it with a smirk.

"Seriously? What poor bastard did she dig her claws into now?"

"His name is Nathan Barnett, and he is definitely not poor. And very handsome."

"Clearly, he isn't smart if he's with Ivy, the biggest gold

digger in Kentucky." I really have no like at all in my body for that woman. I have seen her tear through men since we were children. As a little girl, she used to entice the little boys into her corner by lifting her skirt and winking her third eye at them. I cringe just thinking about it.

"Well, whatever he is, he is good-looking for sure."

"Even more so than your little out-of-town fling the other night?" I tease her, but the truth is, I'm a little jealous. It's been a long time since I had a one-night stand, let alone sex of any kind. It's not that I can't get it; it's just that I haven't had the desire for it lately.

"MMM..." She hums and says, "He is way hotter than... what was his name?

Mark? Mike?"

"Matt," I say, laughing before taking a sip of my second glass of bourbon. "Right. Matt. He was definitely hotter in that suave, sexy, masculine man way."

I don't even know where to go with that, and maybe it's the alcohol, but I have the sudden urge to confide my deepest, darkest secret to her. "Harper..." I say and wait for her to look at me. Once she does, I notice that today she isn't wearing any make-up. Not even the light, glowy, natural stuff she often puts on for her more quiet days. There is a light smattering of freckles across the bridge of her nose, and a light pink blush on her cheeks, mostly from the alcohol. But what strikes me most about her look today is the way the sun lights up her hair from behind, giving it an almost golden fire-like glow. I whisper, "I killed my uncle in this very spot."

With an audible gulp, she swallows the bourbon that she has in her mouth and just stares at me with slightly parted lips.

Chapter Six
Harper

It takes my mind a moment to process the words that just came out of Shelby's mouth, *"I killed my uncle in this very spot."* It's surely a joke. I mean, I know her uncle died when she was what, eleven? Twelve? "Um… that's funny," I say with one of those fake laughs that people give when they don't know if they should laugh or run away screaming. "Tell me another one."

"I also killed my mother."

Now that one makes me laugh out loud. Hard. I throw back the rest of my bourbon and stand up to face Shelby, who is still sitting on the pile of hay bales. "Seriously, Shelb, you have a sick sense of humor sometimes, but man…"

"I'm not kidding." She says it so seriously I cut my laughter off and stare at her again, trying to get a sense of what she is thinking. Hoping that she will blurt out that it's all a joke after all, but she doesn't. She is just sitting there staring into her glass of bourbon. *Holy shit.*

"Why?" I ask the question before I can think better of it. I should be walking out the same door I came in. This is definitely not the Shelby Bowman I know, but her next words have me doing otherwise.

"Because she locked me in the attic, beat and tortured me as a child, and let him molest me for eight years."

In one swift move, I rush to a nearby pail just as my stomach heaves in a successful attempt to empty its contents. Staying bent over the pail with my hands on my knees, all I can taste is bile, and the smell is foul, prompting a second wave of the heaving. Once I'm sure I'm done, I wipe my mouth with the back of my hand, very un-ladylike, and snatch the bottle of Baccarat off the hay bale swigging from the open neck.

"I know. It's a lot to process."

"You think!" I spat back at her.

"I'm sorry. I had to tell someone."

"And that someone had to be m…" At this moment, she looks so lost and forlorn; tears quietly drip from her cheeks, making water spots on her jean-clad thighs.

Remembering that this isn't about me, I move back over to the hay bail and sit next to her. Taking her hand in mine, I say, "I'm the one who should be sorry, Shelb. Nobody deserves to be treated like that. Especially not by their family." And then I wrap my arms around her in a tight hug meant to comfort her and make her feel safe with me.

After a few minutes of silence, Shelby moves from my arms and begins to slowly pace around the area in front of where I sit. Refilling her now empty glass, I hold it out to her. She takes it on her pass by me and sips it while she paces. I wait for her to talk, when she's ready.

"After my dad died and my older brother disappeared, my uncle Lincoln came back into town expecting to take over the family business. When he found out that it all went to me in a trust to be administered by my mom, he flipped and went after her." Taking a slow, shaky breath, she continues to say, "He treated her like shit for not doing more to persuade my father out of making me the sole beneficiary to his will…"

"Wait. Soul beneficiary? What about your brother? He hadn't disappeared yet."

"He wasn't my father's biological son, and he knew it." Not giving me any time to process, she continued, "One night he, my uncle, got drunk, beat her up, and raped her. This happened two more times before the sick bitch bargained me for her freedom." Shelby got that far away look in her eyes that people get when they remember something that happened long ago. "I guess she promised him full run of the farm until I either turned eighteen and he had to fight the courts to give him part of the estate, or I died, but he had to leave her alone and let her live in the life to which she had become accustomed. As an extra bonus, she would help him take his anger out on me. So for eight years, she kept me locked up in the attic while she beat me, starved me, and let him... let him molest me."

Dear God in heaven, I couldn't imagine. I wanted to wrap her in another hug, but she kept up her slow pacing and continued, "Sometimes I would sneak out of the attic. There was a loose board in the wall of my room that opened up to the rest of the attic. I found a small vented opening that led onto one of the pitched portions of the roof, which to my luck, met the top of one of the lattices. On the last night, I snuck out of the attic. I came here to this stable and prayed to God to bring my daddy back. Instead, my uncle found me and tried to rape me. I fought so hard to get away from him, and I only slipped through his fingers because he was stupid drunk. I started to run, but even drunk, he was faster than me. He grabbed my ratted ponytail and pulled me back towards him, but not before I grabbed a nearby pitchfork. Spinning around, I thrust it forward, and... I was trying to protect myself. I didn't mean to

51

kill him. It just… when the pitchfork entered his stomach I dropped the handle, he stumbled forward, and the handle got wedged on a knotted board causing the tines to slide further in." With the toe of her muck boot, she cleared away some dirt and hay to reveal a knotted board. "One of the farmhands had heard me screaming and came in to find me and my dead uncle. The police came out, and my mother said that he was drunk and tried to rape her. She claimed self-defense, and the farmhand backed her up. Later she would say she did it to save us from a scandal, but we both knew she wanted leverage over me; if I ever told anyone what she had done, she would tell them I killed my uncle."

"You would have been free from repercussions if she did. You would only have had to tell them your truth."

"I know that now, but I was twelve Harper, I was only a child, and besides, when I was old enough to realize this, It was too late."

"Why was it too late?"

"Because I had just killed my mother."

"I thought they ruled that an accident?"

"Oh, they did. It was ruled an accidental death due to anaphylactic shock. You see, she was quietly suffering from severe chronic pain and couldn't take the only pain reliever, Oxymorphone, which would have helped her, but she was highly allergic to it. Instead, she was taking OxyContin, which did very little for her pain." With a snorted laugh, she continues, "She never got rid of the Oxymorphone. One night, when I was eighteen, she was getting herself hopped up on the OxyContin, but forgot to grab the bottle from her drawer before heading out to the waiting car. She yelled up to me to bring it down when I came. I deliberately grabbed the

Oxymorphone. I used my sleeve-covered hand to pick it up and dropped it into her purse. An hour later, the police showed up to tell me my mother had gone into anaphylactic shock and died. They said that she had somehow mistaken her pain killer bottles and took the wrong one."

"God…" It's only a whispered word, but Shelby asks me if I think he will forgive her.

"I absolutely do, Shelb. He has to." I go over to where she is standing. Facing her, I take her hands in mine and say, "It was all self-defense. All of it, your uncle, your mother, they did horrible things to you, and they deserved the fate dealt to them."

"I should have gone to the police. I should have told them and… I didn't, though. I knew if I went to the police, there was a chance they wouldn't believe me, so I did the only other thing I could to save myself from them forever."

"I know…" Just then, we heard someone calling out for "Ms Barnett-Bowman". Quickly composing ourselves, we both turn around and face the doors to the Stable just as a stern-looking woman in a dark gray pantsuit comes into view.

"There you are, Ms Barnet…"

"What can I do for you, Detective Gaines?" Shelby cuts her off with a false bravado neither one of us is feeling right now.

Looking at me, the officer says, "Ms Harper Lewis-Sheridan, I presume?"

"You presume correctly, but you have me at a slight disadvantage, officer… was it Gaines?"

"It is."

"Again, Detective Gaines, what can I do for you?"

"Oh well… wait, isn't this the barn where your father and

uncle both died?"

What is this bitch doing? Looking over at Shelby, if the officer was hoping for a reaction, she wasn't going to get one, so I say, "Actually, this is a stable, not a barn. There is a difference, and as you already know, yes, this is where they both died. It is so good of you to bring it up, considering this was Russell Bowman's favorite stable; it's also his birthday today, so we were celebrating his life with a drink. I wonder if Chief Saunders knows, what an astute officer he has working for him. Perhaps I should…"

"No need to threaten an officer of the law, Ms Lewis-Sheridan. I am only here to warn Ms Barnett-Bowman that there is a serial killer on the loose in the greater Louisville area."

"Do you think that I don't read the news?" Finally, Shelby snaps out of whatever trance she was in.

"I'm sure as the savvy businesswoman you are, that you do. However, the news outlets haven't been made aware of one detail." We both stand there waiting for a moment before she continues and says, "The killer is targeting women with brown hair, so I suggest you take care when out and about alone."

"Why would you come all the way out here to tell me this detail?"

"Well, for obvious reasons, of course." She then pointedly looks at Shelby's long chestnut brown colored hair. "And to give you this…" She holds out a piece of paper that has been folded in thirds. Shelby reaches out and takes the paper; quickly opening it up, she begins to read, and Officer Gaines says, "It came up during the investigation of your father's death. I thought you might want to know."

"Investigation?" I ask. "I thought he died from a heart

54

attack?"

Sounding farther away than right next to me, Shelby says, "So did I."

"Your father did die from a heart attack, but it was a drug-induced heart attack. The toxicology report showed that he had a high amount of quinidine and ephedra in his system. Someone wanted him dead, and they drugged him into it." When neither one of us says anything because clearly, we are shocked at this news, she continues, "During the investigation, we learned that your father found out that your brother wasn't his biological son..." Once more, she gives a pointed look, but this time it's to the paper in Shelby's hand, "And that he had begun the process to divorce your mother. And then two nights later, he ends up dead."

"You're telling me that my father was murdered and that all this time I thought he..." choking on a sob, Shelby manages to squeak out the word, "Who?"

"I had my suspicions, but there was never an arrest made. We didn't have enough or rather any conclusive evidence to convict anyone. In any case, it doesn't matter now, I suppose."

"Why doesn't it matter now?" I ask.

"Because both of our main suspects have been dead and gone for several years now."

"You suspected my mother and uncle," Shelby says it as a statement instead of a question.

"I did. Yes."

"Why are you telling me this now? Twenty-four years later. Why?"

"Because the case files are going to be converted to digital media and transferred to a long-term storage server. No one will likely ever look at them again. I felt that you deserved to know… and have the evidence of justification." With that, Officer Gaines turns to leave but stops short. Looking over her shoulder, she says, "I would have done the same thing."

She knows. It's the only explanation we could come up with after she left. Officer Gaines knows that Shelby killed her uncle in self-defense, and that she killed her mother by giving her the wrong painkillers. We also concluded that she didn't plan to do anything about it either.

It was another several hours before I felt comfortable leaving Shelby alone at the house where so much tragedy had taken place. We sat under the twin chandeliers in her formal dining room, playing over every scenario in which this could come back to bite her in the ass since someone else, besides the two of us, knew. All of them ended with Shelby spilling the whole sordid story and begging a jury of her peers for mercy. I didn't think it would come to that, though; something told me that Officer Gaines would maintain her silence.

Chapter Seven
Nathan

When I first decided to venture back to Kentucky, I planned to push my sister out of the family business and take on Lincoln Ward-Sheridan in the process. Buying that man out of his family's empire would have brought me so much satisfaction. And then, last night, I learned that my initial reasons for hating the man weren't what I thought they were. Everything was different than it appeared to be in my mind's eye. Thinking back, all those years ago, when I found a folded-up piece of paper in the pocket of my dad's favorite blazer while I stood staring at his coffin, I didn't think anything of it. It wasn't until a few days later when I remembered it was there, that I pulled it out, opened it, and read the words *"Official Paternity Report"* at the top. Apparently, my father wasn't my father in the biological sense of the word. The report didn't state who my biological father was, so I asked my mother, who at the time told me that Lincoln was my father.

She said she was having an affair with him, got pregnant, and he wanted nothing to do with me. To save face, she kept it a secret for nearly ten years, but then my father found out and threatened to disown us both. She continued to spin her lie by saying that Lincoln and my father got into a fight over it, and that's when he had his heart attack, and Lincoln left him there in the stables to die, doing nothing to save him. Now I know the truth that he was murdered by either my mother, my biological father, who at the time was the man I knew as "uncle", or possibly both.

Standing outside the window of the Stable listening to Shelby and Harper talk was the hardest thing I have ever done in my entire life. So many times, I wanted to jump through the opening and announce my presence and my reasons for being there at that moment.

I was driving through the staff parking lot headed towards the private residence gates when I noticed Harper walking towards one of the farthest stables from the main facility with a bottle in her hand. My curiosity got the better of me, so I parked and quickly made my way through the property, following her at a distance. When she reached her destination, and I realized she was meeting Shelby there, I had planned to announce my presence since I was there to see Shelby anyhow. However, the mention of Ivy's name stopped me; then Harper was talking about me, and then Shelby dropped the bombshell about our uncle and all of the shit she suffered at their hands after I left. There was no going back at this point; I moved around the stable to get better vocals and maybe a visual. Luckily, I moved at the right time because Officer Gaines showed up only moments later, producing a piece of paper, the contents of which I already knew.

Earlier that day, the DNA report I had been waiting on to prove that Lincoln Ward-Sheridan was my father showed up. Instead of confirming my mother's claims, they refuted them. There was no way that Lincoln Ward-Sheridan was my father; however, my deceased uncle was. I had also sent in Shelby's DNA to prove that we were half-siblings, and I was actually the brother who had run away so many years before. Except it showed that we were related genetically more than half-siblings would be. I immediately called my geneticist, who explained that this type of genetic relation could only happen when two people share the same mother and paternal genetic pattern of two different males; in other words, brothers. In simple terms, Shelby and I are not only half-siblings but also cousins. I wanted to join Harper in filling that bucket up.

Blessedly, Tom pulls up in front of the little bistro where Lincoln Ward-Sheridan and I are supposed to meet. Finally free from my thoughts, I make my way through the open double French doors; this place is like a living jungle. The other two outer walls are made up of French doors separated by six-foot sections of wall, six in total, and all of them open. In the openings, there are plant boxes full to overflowing with multi-colored flowers and draping vines. All of the dark green walls are covered with various hanging plants that also cover portions of the ceiling. The only non-plant covered surface is the black and white checkered tile floor. Wall sconces and chandeliers let off only a little bit of light so as to not take away from the beauty of the natural light in this fresh air space, which smells of lavender.

Following the hostess to a table in the corner where the two outer walls meet, I see that Lincoln is already here, accompanied by Harper, who looks even more breathtaking than she did the other night. The two of them are in a deep, whispered conversation when we approach. They are quick to separate when I offer a greeting, "Lincoln, thank you for meeting me here today."

Standing, he offers me his hand while saying, "Of course, I am intrigued to hear your proposal." Motioning for me to take a seat, he takes his own and continues to say, "I hope you don't mind, but I have brought my Chief Environmental Affairs Officer since this is her area of expertise after all. Of course, she is also my daughter." He finishes that off with a wink and chuckle.

Before I can mention it, Harper says, "Actually, we have already met."

"Oh?"

"Yes." I say, "We have a mutual friend and bumped into one another at dinner the other night."

"Very well then. Shall we order drinks?"

It doesn't take long for the business talk to follow the niceties and pleasantries that usually start most business meetings. When I realized that I couldn't come in here and intimidate and bribe the man into selling me his family business, I had to come up with a more legal, above-board, reasonable, and legitimate business opportunity. Or admit that I was planning to ruin him with information that turned out to be false. I'm always in favor of a lucrative business venture.

"Sheridan Reserve already harnesses more than eighty percent of its power source from recycled waste and other biomass. We derive one hundred percent of the water used in our product from the distillery itself. It's naturally filtered underground, iron-free and mineral-rich. Add to that the fact that we have a native grass restoration program, compost ninety-eight percent of our waste, including human waste with compostable toilets, and only serve grown-on-site, pesticide, and GMO-free food in our restaurants and bistro. It's no secret that we already have the cleanest footprints in the industry."

Harper is thinking and talking circles around me, and it's giving me a raging hard-on. My proposition to make Sheridan

Reserve the world's foremost clean energy distillery through hydroelectric power is quickly becoming a moot point since they already are, and I already knew this. "That doesn't mean that you shouldn't consider shoring up that industry lead by being able to also tout a one hundred percent renewable AND clean footprint."

"Correct me if I'm wrong, but hydroelectric power, while clean, can also affect the environment around it. Think natural sediment placement in the rivers, consequently affecting the build-up and maintenance of the land. Also, migratory fish patterns directly affect both terrestrial and aquatic ecosystems. Then there are water overages and shortages in one county or another depending on where the river is dammed and the hazards of a drought. Not to mention it is extremely expensive to build at roughly six hundred dollars per kilowatt. Sheridan Reserve would need between fifteen and twenty-five Mila watts, which would cost us an estimated eight and a half to fourteen and a half million dollars. At that point, we would be better off supplementing the other twenty percent of our power source through solar or wind energy. Add to all of that the potential for Sheridan Reserve to look like a company with a hypocritical view for protecting the environment around us."

"Well, then I'm glad I didn't buy that old Hydro-powered dam yet." What else was I going to say? This was a Hail Mary at best. I had nothing to offer them in the way of a business proposal, and I was not going to admit my original intention to either one of them.

"It was a good thought. Perhaps you can help us work on the way to supplement that twenty percent deficit with solar?"

This is the first time Harper has let Lincoln in on the conversation. Or at least the first time he wanted to chime in.

I suspect that he enjoys watching his daughter chew people up and spit them out. "Solar?"

"That's right," he says. "We have been spit-balling ideas for a few months now and haven't come up with anything concrete. The problem is aesthetic. Solar panels aren't visually pleasing on some surfaces that are at eye level or built on the ground like a farm, and the roofs of most of our buildings are built specifically to accommodate certain temperatures. If we start fortifying those roofs to hold the weight of numerous panels, we throw off the distillation process, thereby tainting our product."

"Let me contact my head of environmental affairs. He recently worked on a small solar farm project in Brunei, which is mostly comprised of dense rain-forested areas. The buildings there have delicate roof structures, and I know keeping the aesthetic appeal was a top priority." After that, the conversation flowed easily back into social niceties and an invite to the Ward-Sheridan annual Derby party. Harper was pleasant but remained mostly silent until we all exited the bistro together.

"It was lovely seeing you again, Nathan."

I take Harper's proffered hand and respond, "Likewise. I look forward to seeing more of you around town."

Chapter Eight
The Cave

Look at them. Sitting there all nice and pretty in their expensive clothes and watches. I can play that game now too. It makes me sick that it all just comes so naturally to him. Everything and everyone just flocks into his fold, and they stay there for the benefits; money, power, sex. I wonder how she would feel if she knew what his original plans for her were. Would she look at him when she knows he's not looking at her? Does she imagine what it would feel like to have his hands slide up her thighs, parting them, teasing her pretty little cunt with his long fingers?

Look at him, practically drooling over her in her black silk blouse and cream-colored pencil skirt. She really is quite stunning in her appearance, almost as much as she is in her beauty alone. The way she moves is graceful, measured, and with intent. Such comfort in her own skin; it's beautiful and makes me want more. She's looking at her father while he speaks; her low ponytail exposes the long lines of her neck with its delicate, creamy skin, the pulse of life rushing beneath it. Oh, to feel that against my lips.

He is desperate for them to allow him into their inner sanctum, if not to ruin them, then to bask solely in her magnificence. I don't blame him really; she is brilliant, eloquent, and above reproach. She commands respect, loyalty, and effort in every aspect of her life and relationships. Unlike most people, unlike me, people genuinely like her.

The way people respond to her, it's sickening but enviable.

Right now, she is giving him a lesson in prior, proper research before daring to waste her time with chump change offers of supremacy when she is already there, when she has already gotten them there. As expected, her father is drawn into his magnetism, though. He is weak and pitiful at best for that. He should know how incredibly lucky he is to have her by his side at the helm.

Maybe I should remove her from this pedestal that I have placed her on, but she has earned it. I love her. Her entire life, she has worked for what she has been given outside of her birthright. I am her witness. In so many ways, she is lucky beyond measure. There are so many reasons that I want to scratch the itch of adoration for her skin to be under my lights, her body on my stage, captive and pliable. But I refuse; I cannot taint the collection of my sacred works with her perfection.

I can no longer sit here and watch this spectacle. Standing and moving silently without notice from either of them, which would prove to be a disaster; it would surely ruin my plans. I make my way to the sidewalk just outside the glass French doors, standing there for a moment with my back to the opening. I look up into the dark sky dotted with tiny little flecks of light, *Lucy in the sky with diamonds*. Thinking of the song lyric that serves as our own private inside joke makes me smile.

The streets around me are bustling with people and cars headed in all manner of directions and places. It's time to find my guest for the evening, someone even more special than usual. Where oh where could she be? I begin to walk down the sidewalk not in any particular direction, but towards someplace a little less popular and a little more... *I spy with my little eye...* more.

It doesn't take me long before I come across an innocuous bar full of college co-eds looking to have more fun than they should, more fun than they can safely handle. But why, oh why are there so many blondes? I'm sure the drapes don't match the carpet on all of them, but there is no time, and I don't have the inclination to find out. Besides, a blonde would be a blemish upon my collection, a false representation of who they really are to me. And yet, I'm oddly turned on by one in particular. She stands with her back against the bar, arched slightly to accentuate the small set of her breasts. She wears a too-short skirt and a cropped top that barely covers her torso; it looks more like a tube top than anything. At first glance, she appears to be yet another blonde, but upon closer inspection, I see that she is, in fact, a brunette; damn low lighting.

She doesn't move as I approach the bar and take my place on a barstool next to her. Above the smell of cheap liquor and sweat, I can smell her light musky fragrance, mixed with a hint of cigarette smoke and shampoo. It's repulsive, really, but only a minor annoyance in the grand scheme of things.

"Excuse me..." I say. She turns only her head and looks at me with a slightly bored expression covered up by a small, fake smile. Clearly, she isn't interested in anything I have to say, but she will be later tonight when we are enjoying one another's company. "Clearly, I have found the wrong bar. Do you know where NachBar is?" I've never actually been there and have no intention to go there, but I do know it's close by, so the question shouldn't seem so out of the ordinary to her. Except instead of answering me, she walks off and disappears into the sea of bleached blonde nothingness.

An hour and a half later, she exits the bar with two other women and a man. From across the street, I can clearly see that they are all drunk to different levels of intoxication; the man and one of the other women more so than my new guest. Following behind them at a safe distance, I have changed from my original evening attire into something a little more functional and comfortable for the next event in my evening activities. I'm glad that I did as they are walking a bit of a distance towards… where I don't know.

Eventually, the man and one woman break off and go in a different direction than my guest and her friend. I'm skimming over scenario after scenario of how to isolate my guest for the taking when they stop in front of a building. The two stand there for a moment having a conversation before her friend stumbles up the stairs into the building, and my guest turns around to dig something out of her purse; a set of keys. With a wink of the lights and an audible click, the locks on a car only a few feet from me set off. This is perfect really, I slow my pace moving closer to the building, and she crosses the street. Just as she opens the door, I swiftly move in, pushing her from behind up against the car, my body firmly against hers. I'm able to plunge my needle into her neck. It only takes a moment for the propofol to kick in. Her body becomes pliable, and I'm able to maneuver her into the backseat of the car before she slumps down hard, totally out.

The drive back to my cave is a long one. I had to choose the perfect location where no one would suspect. It took me years to complete my work. Many lies had to be told to get the funding for such an extravagant chamber, devices of destruction, and a guarantee of privacy. The road down from the top of the rock wall is long and winding with years of overgrowth from the surrounding vegetation, which acts as a perfect cover, keeping the road as hidden as I want it to be. At the bottom, there is an old run-down shack where the caretaker for an abandoned hydroelectric plant on a lock and dam expanding across the rushing river used to live when it was in service. Now, however, it acts as the power supply for my home and showroom. Fortunately, this place is remote enough that no one comes here except for the occasional if not rare set of lovebirds looking to rest under the oak tree and picnic in the quiet.

Having transformed the shack into a hidden garage, I pull my guest from the backseat of her car and lay her down on a rolling cart that is padded for her comfort. Into the lift we go, descending deep into the limestone caves beneath the rock wall. It is cool and damp down here, smelling slightly of mold and salt. The occasional wall-mounted motion lights break up the darkness; I made it a point to activate them when we arrived. All that can be heard besides the *drip drip drip* of water echoing in the open space around us is the crunching of the cart's wheels while I push her along, getting closer and closer to her final destination.

The anticipation I feel as our time together draws nearer is indescribable. It takes all of my carefully harnessed control to keep from stopping this cart and starting my ministrations now. But I'm not adequately prepared. There are processes that must be followed, protocols in place for my safety as well as hers. No, I must wait.

After only a few more minutes, we arrive at my place of worship; it is time to begin. First things first, after I'm sure that she is still safely sleeping, I change from my street clothing into my latex bodysuit covering everything except my eyes and holes for my nostrils and mouth. In the shower she goes, time to wash any trace of me and her earlier activities from her body. This process is always the most extravagant for them; unfortunately, they are never awake to enjoy it. Scalding hot water to wash away their sins and foaming soap to cleanse their soul. There is no need to dry her body after I have scrubbed her to a sparkling perfection; she will air dry center stage until I'm ready for her to wake. This one is special, as she has the ultimate pleasure of my obsessive behavior for Harper focused on her tonight.

She wakes easily once I have introduced enough epinephrine into her system. As usual, her survival instincts kick in shortly after she realizes that she is naked, cold, and shackled to a hard surface. I watch her from several feet above; I'm in the shadows on the steps directly across from where she is on my table. She can't see me, but I can see her arching her body off the table, twisting and turning frantically, trying to free herself, straining so much that her silent grunts turn into screams of terror. She can't see anything outside of the spotlight that is focused on her, not even the beauty of the chandeliers directly above her. Perhaps I will allow her a view of them. Yes, I think I will.

Switching off the spotlight with my remote control, I thrust us both into a momentary darkness. This sends her into a panic, and she begins to scream as if her life depends on it. Well, it does, but it's not necessary. To quiet her shrill cries, I slowly bring up the interior lighting and then switch on the chandeliers. As expected, they catch her attention, and their beauty transfixes her. I lean forward from the shadows causing the metal staircase to creak slightly. This sends her into a chant... "Hello... Hello... Is someone there? P... please. Hello?" No one here is going to help you, my dear.

My movement catches her eye while I descend the stairs with slow, measured steps to the platform. Once there, she notices my attire and begins to beg for her life, "PLEASE... HELP ME! PLEASE DON'T DO THIS!" Her cries continue when I step onto the platform at her feet. "Please don't do this... P... P... Plea..." Her choked cries do nothing but turn me on even more. With a click, I release the platform brake and pivot the table, so she is facing me; her breasts are at my eye level. Her eyes are squeezed shut, and she is muttering something. Is that...? listening closer, I realize she is saying the Lord's Prayer over and over, hoping that he will scoop in and save her from the big bad wolf.

She is destined for disappointment.

Her skin, still a light pink from her bath, is smooth and almost a light caramel.

Not creamy in the slightest, too many years of neglect and sun-worshipping. I run my fingertips along the outside of her thigh, and she trembles from fear. Does she not know that I plan to worship her body? Before I can make another move, she spits in my face. She's a cheeky bitch, so I backhand her hard across the face. The sound of my latex-gloved hand connecting with her skin makes a beautiful *snap*-like sound that echoes for a second before I follow it with another to her other cheek. She is hysterically crying now. Good, the energy from her fear makes me tingle all over, the apex between my thighs becomes warm from my own juices releasing. *Yes...*

It's time to start. Moving the table back into a laying position lowered to the floor enough that I can lean over her body while I do my work. I search for the perfect patch of skin to place my signature. Ah yes, right there on her lower abdomen just to the left of her belly button. It doesn't take me long to fetch the waiting poker and return to her side. She feels better with me in her sights than where she can't watch me. This is evident from her lessening cries. She is watching me intently with her piercing green eyes; it intrigues me, and I find myself watching her with my head cocked slightly to the side. She isn't making any noise, but as I lift my hand, showing her the hot poker, she weeps again, asking me to please not hurt her. I place my hand on the spot I intend to mark. She begs, and I begin to cut into her skin; blood sizzles and skin melts, mingling with the scent of her tears and fears, creating a euphoric high like no other.

Chapter Nine
Nathan

Tom never showed up when I paged him after my dinner with Lincoln and Harper, so here I sit, in the backseat of a smelly cab paying way too much for a ride home. It's not like him to no-show like that. If he's in the middle of something at the house, he usually sends Lee in his place. As we pull up to the house, I notice the gate is closed. Rather than have the taxi driver enter my security code, I pay the man, and when he pulls away, I head to the wicket door, enter my code and push it open. With a click, it shuts behind me, and I head up the circular drive noticing that the car is not in the driveway and all the lights are off. Weird, but I don't think it is weird enough to warrant any sort of worry or fear.

Once I have entered the main foyer of the house, I head to the kitchen, no one. So I peek into the recreational room, no one. Maybe they are in their own quarters? Heading down the back hallway of the house, I go up a short flight of steps and hear noises coming from the other side of their bedroom door. *Holy Shit… I'm not interrupting that.* But just as I'm about to turn away, I hear what sounds like strangled cries coming from someone followed by the crash and shattering of something glass. What I saw when I opened the door was extremely confusing until I realized Tom was dead.

A very naked Lee was still straddling Tom's naked and

motionless body. Tom was lying on his front, his face to the side, eyes wide open with his arm slung over the bed. He must have knocked the crystal lamp onto the floor in the struggle where it shattered into a million pieces. Lee had his palm flat on Tom's back. His breathing was very heavy, and his cock was still partially between Tom's ass cheeks.

"Lee…" I said his name as calmly as I could so as to not startle him, but it didn't work. He jumped at hearing my voice but didn't move otherwise. "Lee…" I said his name again and started to move closer to the bed to check on Tom.

"I… I don't know what happened." His voice is hoarse and cracks once he starts to cry.

"Okay, why don't you move off him, and I'll check for a pulse, all right?" He nods his head and moves off Tom's body. I push the gravity of this situation aside as I try to palpitate around on Tom's neck for a pulse and come up empty. I lift his wrist, nothing. Fuck… "He's dead."

"I should have stopped. I just… I just got carried away and now… now…" He breaks into body-jerking sobs.

Running through the list of scenarios to fix this shit show, calling the police is not one of them. Lee would surely go to jail for life. It was an accident, and I'm not going to let him waste away as someone else's bitch in the state penitentiary. "We need to clean this up, Lee." Moving over to where he is now on the floor, I crouch down to eye level and say, "Lee, man, I get that it was an accident, but we need to clean this up before the sun comes up, and then you need to leave town."

"We should call the cops."

He says it so matter of fact that I almost change my mind and agree with him, but instead, I say, "No, we don't. They won't take that it was an accident as a reason. You will go to prison for life, and I can't let that happen over a stupid accident. Okay? Are you going to help me?"

After a moment, he looks me in the eyes and says, "Okay." Before he stands up and goes into the bathroom to hopefully clean up and get dressed, I throw a sheet over Tom's body and set off to find a tarp and some duct tape.

It took less time than I expected to get Tom's body cleaned up from the sex, wrapped in the tarps, and into the back of my Range Rover SVAutobiography Dynamic Black Edition. I watch too many true-crime shows, for sure. The drive out to the spot where we will bury the body takes a lot longer and is eerily quiet. Not that I expect Lee to be chit-chatty, but yeah. Before we left the house, I had him pack a bag, and I grabbed about two hundred thousand in cash from my home safe. He was going to need it where he was going. Looking back, I'm glad I had those fake passports made for all of us just in case.

As we approach the backside of Bowman Farm, I pray that the code to the access gate still works. When I ran away all those years ago, this is the gate I left the property through. For about two days, I hid out in a hollowed tree trunk not far from this gate, thinking about my strategy and eating snacks I had pilfered from the kitchen. I knew I wasn't going to make it on my own unless I had some money and more food. The night before I left for good, I doubled back to the main training facility, stole the cash reserves that I knew were in the auxiliary paddock, and took the stash of snacks that were there for the trainers. It wasn't a lot of money, but it was enough to get me set up somewhere until I could get a plan in motion. The next night, I left the only home I had ever known and never looked back until now.

As we approach the gated entrance, I feel hopeful that the code will work, given that the drive is overgrown with weeds and the gate is covered in rust. I throw the SUV in park, and say, "I'll be right back." Getting out of the driver's side, I pull on a pair of black leather gloves and use a pen flashlight from my glove box to look around for any cameras or security equipment. I don't see any, so I move over to the pin pad, brush some dirt and weeds aside and enter the numbers, sending up a silent prayer they work. *BINGO!* The lock clicks, and I begin to push the gate open. This is proving harder than I would have liked. Lee gets out of the SUV and, putting on his own gloves, silently helps me muscle it open through the tangle of weeds, grass, and dirt. Once it's open, we hop back in the Range Rover and drive down the dirt road a few minutes. When the tree I want comes into sight, I park the SUV once again and contemplate leaving the headlights on, facing Tom's final resting spot before I think better of it and shut them off. The likelihood of anyone knowing we are out here is slim to none.

Quietly and in complete synchronization, Lee and I drop two shovels and a camping lantern off by the tree before making a return trip with the body. Belatedly I should have changed before we came out here; the tall grass in the field is damp from the misty late night or early morning air. Whichever way you prefer to think about it. I'm still in my Zegna suit and Alessandro Oxfords from dinner while Lee is in a pair of jeans, a hoodie and work boots, his standard attire.

"Why this tree?" He asks.

Before I answer, I look up into the dark canopy of oak leaves and breath a deep breath. There is a sight chill tonight, but it feels good in my lungs. "This is the tree I hid in when I ran away."

"So it has a special place in your life. Just like Tom does in mine." With that last part having been said, he lifts the shovel up and thrusts it back down, the spade tip cutting into the dirt with the ease of a hot knife going through butter.

It took quite a bit of work and effort, but after about an hour or so, we got the grave completely dug. It was pretty deep too, which was good. It was time to put Tom in, but Lee just stood there staring at the lump of tarp and human flesh. It's tragic, really. The two of them hav... had something amazing. Most people never manage to find their best friend and lover in the same person, but Lee did. Remembering when I first met them, they weren't officially married, and they were small-time burglars, but clearly loved one another in a manner that made me envy them. After a year of working with them on several projects, they got married, and I brought them on as full-time employees. Not only did they help me with my properties and such, but they also took care of some other less domestic situations. There is no doubt that I am going to miss them both very much.

Maybe someday Lee can come back, but for the foreseeable future, it's best if he disappears.

"Ready?" I ask him.

"Ready." He says before bending over to lift one end of the tarp while I bend over to lift the other. We sidestep in unison to the long edge of the grave and swing the body over the opening, both of us letting go. The body hits bottom with a loud *THUD*. I close my eyes and cringe. Lee lets off a choked sob.

"What do you two think you're doing out here?" It's a very distinct female voice belonging to Shelby Barnett-Bowman. We both slowly turn to face her. She has a flashlight pointed at us and a shotgun in her other hand.

"Shelby…" I say her name to her for the first time since we were children. "This isn't what it looks like."

Her eyebrows lift in a knowing manner. "You mean you aren't out here burying something on my property? And how do you know me?"

"Because I'm your brother, Nate."

Chapter Ten
Shelby

Did this guy just say he was my brother? "I'm sorry. Come again?"

"I ran away from home when you were two years old, right after Dad... well, your dad died."

"That's all, public knowledge. What am I'm supposed to believe you because you're out here burying a dead body?"

"We don't have the same father. Your dad found out I wasn't his just a few days before he died of an apparent heart attack. And I have proof."

"Let's see it. And who's this?" I ask while pointing the shotgun at the other man.

"He is a friend of mine. His name is Lee."

"And who was that?" This time I lift my chin towards the grave. "That's my husband, Tom." Lee answers before Nate can.

"Jesus Christ. You're seriously out here burying a dead body? How the fuck did you get in the gate?" That gate hasn't been used in years. And only my foreman and I know the access code.

"The access code was never changed from when we were kids and used to play out here at this tree."

He watches me while my brain wheels turn, remembering all of the times nanny would bring us out here to play children's games, until she made us go back to the house. "Where's this proof?"

"It's in my briefcase in the backseat of the Range Rover."

Taking a minute to think over my next move, I say, "Which side?"

"Passenger's."

"Do not move, or I will add both of you to Tom's grave." Moving backwards, I keep my eyes on both of them, and my shotgun pointed in their general direction. It's a good thing they have no clue it's not loaded. When I reach the back door of his SUV, I open the door, pull out his black leather briefcase and walk back over to where the two men stand. Setting it down on the ground, I open it and peer inside.

"It's in the blue folder."

I pull the blue folder out. Standing back up, I move the briefcase aside with the toe of my foot, stick the end of my flashlight in my mouth, gross. It tastes like metal and dirt. But I need to hold it while I open the folder and pull out the paperwork, which reads "*Official Paternity Report*" at the top. The following verbiage is all a bunch of this and that, with the basic gist showing that we are brother and sister, or at least from the same mom. "Nate," I say his name looking at his face for some sign of the eight-year-old boy I once spent every day with. He is a man now for sure, but is he really... "It's really you?"

"It is."

"What does this other part mean. The part about two different genetic males?"

"It means that we share the same mother and paternal genetic pattern of two brothers."

This is insane. I knew he was only my half-brother, but

does this mean, "Uncle was your father?"

"Yes."

"How long have you known?" I ask him because I only just found this out yesterday, and only the part about him not having the same dad, among other things.

"Only the other day."

"You got a sample of my blood for a blood test? How…" He cuts me off and explains that it was actually a saliva sample from my glass at the dive bar I went to earlier in the week. The one I visited after my therapist. "You've been following me? For how long?"

"Not long, seriously, I just got here with Lee and T… I was making a plan to approach you. And this…" Looking around, he finishes with, "Is not it."

"Can we finish this before it gets to be light out, please?" Lee is ridiculously calm for a guy who is about to bury his dead husband.

"You're going to need about a hundred pounds of lye to dissolve that body, and I didn't see any in your SUV." *Jesus Christ. What am I saying?*

"You don't happen to have any we can borrow, do you?" Nate asks and then quickly says, "Forget I asked that…"

"You're in luck. It's back at the main facility, though." They both stand there looking at me like I have ten heads. "What? We use it for when we have to bury a stillborn foal. Or when a horse dies during bir… Why am I explaining this to you two? I'm not the one who killed a man, and now…" The forlorn sadness that comes over Lee's face stops my tirade and breaks my heart. I put everything but my flashlight down, walk over to him and wrap him a huge hug around his middle. "I'm sorry for your loss," I whisper. It takes a moment, I probably freaked him out, but he hugs me back and lays his cheek on top of my head.

"Why don't you tell me where it is, and I will go get it."

Stepping back from Lee's loosening embrace, I say, "I'll go with you. If someone sees you in there, especially dressed like that, they are definitely going to call security."

Lee promises to wait with Tom's body while we go get the lye, and we promise to make it quick. It shouldn't take us long if we take the SUV and follow the dirt road into the main pastures, then into the training facility area. Once there, we only need to grab two fifty-pound bags, and we will be on our way back in a jiffy, in theory anyhow.

"How did you get out here?" Nate asks as we pull away from the tree and start towards the main pastures.

"I rode a horse."

"Where did it go?" He starts looking out the windows as if he could see it in the dark fields around us.

"She's probably already back in the main pasture area."

"Okay. How did you know…"

I cut him off this time, and with a heavy sigh, I say, "You tripped the alarm I had installed on that gate about five years ago." I continue to explain that after our mother died and I took over full control of Bowman Farm, I made several facility upgrades, and security was one of them.

"Good call." He responds.

"Where have you been all these years? Why did you leave?" I have to know. I'm so confused right now. Part of me feels like I should hate him for leaving me at the mercy of our mother and his father. The rest of me wants to jump for joy having the only family, besides Harper, back in my life.

"I left because I found the papers saying I wasn't your full brother. And Mom told me Lincoln was my father and that…"

"Lincoln! As in Lincoln Ward-Sheridan?" I'm shocked and don't know where to process that info.

"Yes. She also told me he was the reason your dad had a heart attack.

She said they were fighting, and he just left him there to die."

"But that's not what…"

"I know."

"How do you know? Do I want to know how you know?"

"I was on my way to see you yesterday when I saw Harper walking towards one of the stables, so I followed her and…"

"You heard everything." I feel like I'm going to throw up. He knows about…

"I did. And I won't say anything to anyone. They both deserved what they got." Neither one of us says anything for a few moments. I don't know what he is thinking, but I know I'm freaking the fuck out right now. The only person who was supposed to know was Harper, and now Nate… Is this really Nate?

Looking over at him, I try to see that little boy again, but my mind just remembers him as well as I used to. But I do see my uncle and mother in him. Suddenly he says, "Besides, now you have leverage on me." He's referring to Tom.

"Did you do it"

"No. Lee did. It was an accident."

I don't say anything to this. It is none of my business. "Follow the road to the left. It's the smaller barn over there." I say, pointing to the one I'm referring to.

Once we pull up in front of the dark red barn, we both get out of the SUV, and he follows me to the sliding doors. I tell him we need to be quiet while moving the doors to glide open easily, as they should, given that it's one of the newer barns it hasn't had time to stiffen up.

Inside we move quickly to the back storage area. Currently, there are only three pregnant mares in this barn, so it's quiet, given that they have already been fed and tucked in for the night. Becky, the night nurse, is hopefully sound asleep in the adjoining office/apartment area. These mares aren't set to deliver for another week, so there isn't any reason for her to come out here.

The storage room doors are locked, and it takes me a minute to find my passkey, but once I do, I swipe it in front of the lock, which allows the doors to pop open. Inside, it's ridiculously dark, so I turn on my flashlight, not wanting to turn on the overhead lights and disrupt the sleeping mares. We locate the lye and each grab a bag. Fifty pounds is way heavier than I anticipated. I struggle with the bag and the flashlight, so Nate takes the light, and we move back through the open doors. Nate is able to maneuver the doors closed quietly, even with the fifty-pound bag in his arms. Show off.

Making it back to the SUV, we place the lye bags in the back and get in the front seats. Starting the Range Rover, Nate navigates us back to where Lee is. When we get there, he is sitting on the ground next to the grave. His back is against the tree trunk, his arms folded over his chest, and his head is tipped downward. I know he's asleep because he startles awake when we shut our doors.

I stand back and watch as the two of them dump the lye on top of Tom's body, followed by all of the dirt and strips of grass they had removed to dig the hole. I have to admit I'm impressed they thought to do that; I would have just dug a hole with no regard to the remaining dirt mound that was left. I suppose it's a good thing I didn't have to cover up my murders. *For the love of God…*

I'm going to burn in hell!

As the sun begins to rise in the east, we pull away from the curb at the local bus stop where we dropped Lee off. I guess he plans to take the money, and new passport that Nate gave him and head into Mexico, then the Maldives from there. It's a solid plan, I think. If I were going to flee to a non-extradition country, I would want sandy beaches and warm water too.

"I'll take you back to the farm now. If you want?"

"How about breakfast first? Being an accessory to murder makes me hungry." It's not funny, but it really is, so we both laugh at the stupidity of what we just helped a man do.

Chapter Eleven
Harper

From my vantage point, atop a large hill on the back of Dutch, my Akhal-Teke, I can tell it's going to be a beautiful Kentucky morning. I reach down and stroke my gloved hand across Dutch's long muscled neck. He is a Turkish thoroughbred with a coat that shines like spun gold in the early morning sunlight. Dutch was a gift from my grandfather when I turned twenty-five; he said it was the perfect gift to celebrate a quarter of a century's worth of life. He was right. He died three months later from colon cancer. I miss him every day.

Looking out over the countryside ahead, the rolling green pastures, bisected by dark wooden fencing, sprawl out in a perfect carpet leading to the backside of my family's estate. Green trees of every possible shade and height haphazardly form groups along the open space, almost like gossiping grandmothers at a wedding. Over it all, there is a low-lying mist that provides the perfect filter for the rays of the sun, which later will provide us all with a warmth to wrap around our shoulders like a cozy blanket on a chilly winter's morning.

As the sky lingers in its golden yellow-orange hue before turning to the light blue of the day, I feel my cell vibrate against the side of my thigh. No doubt it is the office looking for my signature on some document for Sheridan Reserve, or maybe it's my mother looking for me to confirm my dress choice for tomorrow night's Derby party. Of course, there is a chance it's someone looking to say hello to me. No business. No party stuff. But then it's too early for all of that to be possible. I reach down and unzip the utility pocket on the side of my dark gray jods and pull my phone out. The screen displays a missed call and a text message from Shelby. Sliding my thumb up on the screen, it processes my facial recognition and opens up to the main screen. In my messages' app, I open the text from Shelby, asking me to call her as soon as possible. What could she possibly have to tell me at this hour of the day? This thought prompts me to think about our conversation the other night. The one where she told me that not only was she abused and tortured by her mom and uncle, but that she also killed them both. I can't even fathom what she has gone through in her lifetime, from losing her father and brother at such a young age to being a sexual plaything for her own uncle. It's disgusting, and the thought of it makes me want to be sick all over again.

I put my phone back in my pocket and roll my shoulders underneath my black Italian Barchetta Baby Cashmere sweater and find myself thinking more and more about what I would have done in her position. It's not that I fault her or blame her, but what must a person be thinking about to take another person's life? Are they thinking at all? These two people, two people she should have been able to trust with the care of her person and life, completely let her down. There is not a doubt in my mind that they both belong in hell, but prison... no. She did the right thing. If anyone ever hurt me in the way that they hurt her, I would do whatever I had to in order to protect my future and myself, even if that meant committing murder. Blessedly, I have never been in that situation. It breaks my heart for her, and I hope she knows that

I don't judge her for her past or her actions. Not one bit.

As if he can hear my disturbing thoughts, Dutch begins to grow restless underneath me. No doubt, he is eager to make his way back to his warm stall in the stables, where he will get a thorough grooming and some feed lined with chaff. Pulling on the leather reins in my hands, we begin with a slow trot before Dutch works his way into a jog, then eventually into a full-on gallop.

His mane flows loosely in the dewy air around us, and I can feel the shorter hairs of my curtain bangs coming loose from the messy bun I put my hair in this morning. The biting chill of the morning feels good on the exposed skin of my face; it burns my throat with each inhaled breath. This is the most freedom I have felt in longer than I can remember. With all of the chaos of my life, these stolen moments in the wide-open space of this place I call home is perfection, and it isn't long until I pull back on the reins and bring Dutch back to a slow trot as we near the stables that he knows as home.

There is a slight undertone of hay and manure beneath the scent of fresh-cut grass and peonies when we trot into the main paddock. Ahead of us, Dutch's trainer steps into the opening of the stable doors, likely prepared to take the reins from me, untack, groom, and feed Dutch. Some days I like to do it myself; others, I let the trainer do it. Today I prefer to let the trainer do it. Unfortunately, I have other things to do today, starting with a shower.

Three hours later, I am pulling out of the employee parking lot at the corporate headquarters building for Sheridan Reserve. The intent was to go into the office to take care of the stack of paperwork on my desk; that was before I got called into the distillery for a private tour. It's always a joy when the billionaire Arab Sheiks come into town for the races with their multiple wives and entourages. This particular Sheik was one of the youngest I've ever met, and I've definitely met my fair share. In his mid-forties, handsome in a distinguished and gentlemanly manner, he spoke English with more of a British accent than that of his fellow cohorts. It was refreshing that he didn't think about asking me to become one of his wives, as they often do. Why, I have no idea. I definitely do not play into the submissive wife role that shares her husband.

I turn left onto the long road leading up to the parking lots for Bowman Farm and the gated drive for the private family residence where Shelby grew up and still lives. The large wrought iron gates are open, likely because she knows I'm on my way. Her long driveway looks much like mine and that of every other rich Kentucky resident, long, straight, lined by wooden fencing, shrubs, flowers, and coming to an end at a circular drive, in front of the family home. Shelby's triple-level home has a red brick façade with tall white columns that support the balcony and portico for the second and third floors. Huge windows across the front of the home look like orderly soldiers waiting for inspection, and a double door white front entry with a half-circle arch of windows above it is slightly ajar. It seems a bit odd, but there is also a blacked-out Range Rover with an open back hatch parked there, maybe more than a bit odd.

Putting my silver Bentley Bentayga in park behind the other SUV, I open my door, and between the soft, supple leather of the seat and my leather leggings, I slide out with a cool, practiced ease. A soft thud behind me signals the closing of the driver's side door. I walk towards the path leading to the front porch, except the tapping of my black sued Jimmy Choo peep-toe stiletto heels on the brick of the driveway comes to a quick stop when I notice a plastic bag about to fall out of the back of the Range Rover. I like to consider myself a nice person, so I take the few steps towards the SUV and take hold of the empty plastic bag with my free hand…

"Harper! You're here already."

Looking back towards the house, I see Shelby walking down the front steps, Nathan Barnett behind her. Interesting. "Yeah, I just got here. This bag was falling out of the boot, so…"

She cuts me off quickly and nervously says, "Yeah, just leave it there.

"It's fine. I got it."

"Really," I say with a laugh, "It's fine. I can bring it into the trash."

"NO! I… I mean, I wouldn't want you to get any residue on your clothes." She says, reaching for the bag.

"Residue? What is it…?" I ask as I also lift the bag to see the name of the product it once contained. *Lye.* "Lye? Did one of the horses die?" I ask, looking towards the stables and the farm.

"Uh… yeah. One of the mares had a stillborn."

"Uh huh." Shelby is acting weird. "Hello, Nathan. I didn't know you two knew each other?"

The two of them look back and forth between themselves, and then Nathan says, "Yeah, it's a long story for sure."

"Great. You two can explain it to me after you explain why you are transporting empty lye bags in the back of your SUV and into the house." My daddy didn't raise no fool.

For the second time in a matter of only days, I am again processing a bomb of information dropped on me by Shelby and this time also Nathan. The two are siblings. Apparently, Nathan is her long-lost brother who ran away when he was only ten years old after their dad died, and he found out that he wasn't actually his biological dad. The details just keep coming after that revelation. From what I gather, Nathan ran away to Seattle, where he was living the thug life of a street hooligan, stealing and mugging people. Before one night when he tried to mug a lone woman who, to his surprise, beat the crap out of him and then "adopted" him into her life and home. He became a changed boy from that day on, got an education, and started his own business buying and selling small properties once he flipped them. When he was seventeen years old, his adopted mom, who had no other family, passed away, leaving him everything she owned. Including the fortune, he never knew she had. After a series of wise investments, his business grew and took off into the multi-billion-dollar industry monster that it is now. It sounds like one of those too good to be true Cinderella stories of rags to riches, which it is. It's hard to believe that this man is the little boy in all of the pictures around the house.

Turns out that he also knows about everything Shelb and I talked about in the barn that night, both alone and with Officer Gaines. While I'm incredibly happy for Shelb, that she has her once beloved brother back, I'm skeptical about his timing especially given that he is trying to enter into a joint energy conversion venture with Sheridan Reserve. Again, it turns out that he was under the impression that he and I shared the same father... Thank God, we don't. I would feel sick knowing that I was thinking the dirty things I was thinking about Nate if he was, in fact, my brother, but he's not.

"So yeah, the other night, I was all thumbs as I tried to pull a probable business venture out of my ass in place of my original plan to run the man who abandoned me and killed the only man I knew of as my father. Which was, as we all know, not the case." He says it with a true look of regret on his face.

"Well, it wasn't that bad of a pitch, just... definitely a little off the mark. Besides, you got the verbal to help with solar, so there's that."

I refrain from asking the question that I really want to ask and instead say, "Now tell me what's up with the lye?"

"A horse died."

"We helped bury a dead man."

They both spoke at the same time, so I didn't quite catch what Shelby said until my brain processed all of the words along with the shocked stare Nate was now giving her, and the wide-eyed expression of being caught in the act she was giving me. "I'm sorry," I say, laughing almost manically, "It sounded like you said that you helped bury a dead man."

"Yup."

Nate adds on by saying, "We definitely did."

Why is it that lately, every time I have a conversation with Shelby, she confesses murder or, in this case, her accessory to murder after the fact? "Am I the only person in this room who hasn't committed murder?"

"No. I haven't." Nathan actually raised his hand when he said this.

Dummy.

"Thanks, guys. Way to make a girl feel bad about her sins."

"Shelby, that's not what..."

She cuts Nate off and says, "One of his employees accidentally killed his husband while they were having sex, they broke into the back pasture, and I caught them trying to bury him under the old oak, and yeah. That's when I found out he was my brother, and I just couldn't not help them. You know?"

"No, I don't know, Shelby. Why didn't you guys call the police? If it was an accident, then…"

Nate now cuts me off. "Because they aren't exactly your average upstanding citizens. It was best to do it this way."

"So where is the other one? You know the one who wasn't fucked to death?" They both just look at me like I've lost my ever-loving mind, which I have at this point.

"He is probably halfway to his new non-extradition life status."

"Well, it's never a dull moment these days. That's for sure." I sigh and turn to walk further into the parlor where we are sitting. The room is large and runs the length of about half the house. With light yellow walls, white chiffon drapes, and a mixture of complementary pastel-colored and wood-toned furniture, the sunlight makes it seem like every light in the room is on when it isn't. I let my head fall back on my shoulders, taking in the plaster ceiling, which is sectioned off by crown molding into large squares; so neat and orderly. "How long do you plan to stay in town?" I ask Nathan while looking back at the windows before turning to look at the two siblings standing only a few feet apart.

"I don't have any current plans to leave."

I nod my head in the affirmative, thinking about how good that is for Shelby. Maybe the two of them can get to know one another again. You know, outside of their shared bond with the murder victim. I mentally place my palm over my face. Seriously I couldn't make this shit up if I tried.

Chapter Twelve
Harper

My brain feels like it has just run a marathon outside of my head, on a hot cement path lined with sharp nails, pointy end up. That's the only way I can describe the mental exhaustion from the constant stream of information that is flowing through it right now. So many secrets revealed, so many secrets to keep, so many feelings to hold onto, and so many things I want to say and ask. This is bound to turn into a shit show for sure. Add to that, that another young college girl was found raped, tortured and mutilated to death. Disturbing sounds better than shit show at this point.

Standing in front of my eight-foot-high five-foot-wide mirror, I look at the dress I have chosen to wear to Ivy's party tonight. It isn't the slinky little black number I would prefer to wear, but because it's a Derby party, I chose a blush pink colored custom Naeem Kahn pleated cape sleeve bodycon midi dress. This thing is perfection; it hugs every curve I possess and then some.

I've chosen to pair it with a smoky eye look, the exact same colored Christian Louboutin So Kate heels, and a custom fascinator in the same pink color with roses made of silk, fabric curls, and a large, wide brim tilted slightly off-center. The finished look takes on your classic "pretty in pink" moniker with a subtle undertone of sultry and sexy. I'm in love with it.

"Harper, darling?"

I can hear my mother getting closer to my dressing room doors. She's likely here to tell me that Kenny has arrived and is already hitting the bourbon with Daddy. I laugh at this thought because it's exactly what she says when she walks through the barely open doors. "She never can say no to that man."

"Well, can anyone?" After thirty years of marriage and thirty-eight years of being together, they are both still as much in love with one another as they were the day they met. "You look positively divine."

"You think so? Is the color okay?" I only ask because pink normally isn't my color. With my fair pink-toned skin and strawberry blonde hair, I tend to stick with the neutral tones.

"Yes, I absolutely think it looks amazing. Naeem did a wonderful job on this ensemble."

"I think so too. It's possibly one of my favorites." I say and walk towards her as we both make our way out into my main bedroom space. It's the same room I have slept in since the day they brought me home from that field.

Now, I only stay here on occasion. Often times I stay at my penthouse in the city, which is closer to the office and much quieter. When I'm here, Mom likes to chat me up about this, that, and everything else happening in Kentucky society and around the world. Dad likes to talk shop, horses, and play cards.

Since it's Derby week, I promised her I would stay here for a few days to help with the party and such. Not that there is much for me to do except walk around and make sure all the little worker bees are doing what they should be. I always end up making my way out to the stables or to Dad's home office, where we talk about random nothings until Mom finds us and puts us back to work. It's positively exhausting.

"Whose party is it tonight?" She asks Kenny when we enter the first-floor den.

"Ivy Stallwerth," Kenny says before she throws back the last sip of bourbon in her glass.

"I don't know if I'm familiar with her?" Mother says it with genuine curiosity. She's met her many times before; however, Ivy isn't someone who generally makes a memorable impression on people, except Nathan, that is. I wonder what he sees in her?

"Anyhow, Kenny, are you ready, my love? We have people to meet and places to go."

Three hours later, we met Shelby, Lucy, and Bryan for some pre-party cocktails; the five of us arrive at Ivy's townhouse in downtown Louisville. It's a classic brownstone from the front, modern inside, and there is a spectacular garden area outside walled in and separated from her neighbors, who likely have similar outdoor areas. She chose to buy on Millionaires Row in the historic district, not a bad decision considering these gorgeous homes have been here since the Victorian era, but for the life of me, the constant ghost tours passing by would drive me mad enough to… well, we will just say mad.

Ivy's party planner has done a nice job of decorating tastefully, if not a little bridal shower like, what with the balloon arches, flowers, and is that a champagne tower? "I'll be over there getting champagne." Followed by Lucy and Shelby, we walk smack dab into a photographer who won't take no for an answer. I'm sure it won't be the last picture of the evening, but really? A staff photographer from the Kentucky Herald, overkill for sure.

"Harper, there you are." Ivy appears with the same photographer we just saw and Nathan. "I'm so glad you could all make it. I saw Kendal and Bryan just over there." It's said dismissively with a wave over her shoulder.

"You remember Nathan, don't you?"

"Hello Ivy, and yes, I remember Nathan." I answer and look at Nathan pointedly, "It's so nice to see you again. You've met Shelby, right? And this is Lucy."

"Ladies, it's a pleas…" His is cut off by a frantic Ivy who takes off after a waiter who just dropped a tray outside on the patio

"Gah, what do you see in her?" Shelby asks him. "She's… nice."

Lucy laughs at that before heading back over to where Bryan is standing;

Kenny must have snuck off to the ladies' room. "Well, good luck to you, sir," I raise my glass, feigning a toast before taking my first sip. It's dry and bubbly for sure.

"She isn't that bad, seriously. She idolizes you."

I have to stop myself from choking on my champagne at his words.

"What gives you that idea?" I continue to cough a couple more times, clearing my throat while Shelby laughs at me, the bitch.

"Maybe the way she seeks your attention? Or that this party went from great to hopefully amazing when you said you would show up with 'LKB'." He made air quotes around that last part.

"Then she should seek psychiatric attention." Maybe it's

harsh of me to be as dismissive as I am about his revelation, but Ivy is a nosey, gossipy whore who needs to clean her act up and get a life of her own. With that, I look around for Kenny and spot the back of her brown-haired head by the hallway that leads to the kitchen. "Excuse me, for a moment."

Leaving Shelby and Nathan to their own conversation, I make my way to Kenny, who is talking to some downtown banker type with black hair. He is attractive but not her type. Kenny prefers her men tattooed, wearing leather, and running from the cops.

Sidling up to her, I wrap my arm around her slender waist sheathed in a light blue silk confection, and place a light kiss on her cheek. "There you are," I say, smiling at her. "Who's your friend?"

With a laugh, she responds with, "This is Chet. Chet, this is my friend, Harper."

"Hello, Chet."

"Hello. It's nice to meet you, Harper."

"But is it really Chet?" All of the alcohol I've had to this point is starting to give me that warm fuzzy feeling. As a result, I'm unnecessarily being a bitch.

But he's a good sport and laughs at me before saying, "Oh, it is. Say, are you two just friends or more like lovers?"

"Isn't it rude to ask a woman her sexual preference on the first date?" I ask before Kenny responds.

"Wouldn't you like to know? Come on, Harper, let's go get some air."

With that, we walk away from Chet and head farther down the hallway. Except instead of turning towards the room with the open patio doors, she walks to a closed door on the opposite side of the hallway.

When we enter the room, in the ambient light, it looks to be a library that has barely been used by the current homeowner. While there are books on the shelves, there is little else in the room; only an overstuffed chair and floor lamp. "What are we doing in here?" I ask.

"I thought you could use a minute away from all the people and cameras." That was Kenny for you, always thinking about what is best for me. There are many situations that would have made the front page of the paper and scandalized my family if it wasn't for her. It would be an understatement to say that Kenny isn't only my friend. She is my best friend.

Walking over to one of the book-lined walls, I let my fingertips run from book spine to book spine, making a mental note of all the classic book titles in the collection; Moby Dick, A Tale of Two Cities, Gulliver's Travels, and so on. I wonder if Ivy has even read any of these books. It isn't until Kenny's whispered response in my ear that I realize I spoke the question aloud.

Why is she so close? I start to turn around when she places her hands on my hips, keeping me facing the bookcase. "Kenny, what are you doing?"

"Do you think Nate touches Ivy like this?" When she asks the question, she slides her flat hands around to the front of my dress right over my lady bits.

With a nervous laugh, I say, "I don't actually think about them or what they do when they fuck, Kenny. What is this?"

"This is me appreciating you, Harper." In the next breath, I can feel Kenny's hands slide down my naked legs before she begins to push my dress up.

"Kenny, stop this. It isn't funny." The words are coming

out of my mouth, but my body seems to be frozen in place, but it's not. I try to step away from her, but she has me pinned against the shelves with a hand on my back, the other slides up the inside of my thighs.

"Spread your legs, Harper." It's a command. "Let me in." Kenny keeps sliding her hand upward, forcing it between my thighs until my body betrays me, and my thighs part just enough for her to get her hand exactly where she wants it. Her fingertips make quick work of pushing my tiny silk thong aside before she plunges them deep inside my pussy. Pushing and twisting, I can't help it when my legs spread more for her, giving her more room to move. My breath is coming in rapid gusts timed with her strokes against my clit, I'm trying my hardest not to make a sound, but it's getting harder and harder as she brings me to climax... "Don't make a sound, Harper. We don't need anyone seeing this do we?" She's right. Of course, she's right. She's always right. Why is she doing this? Again, her answer lets me know that I didn't just think the question, "You need to be worshipped, Harper, and I'm going to be the one to do it."

I hadn't even realized that she had backed away from me and left the room until I heard the soft click of the door shutting, followed by only my own breathing. *What the fuck...* I'm frozen in my stance, facing the shelves, when a noise in the hallway followed by people laughing startles me into action. I fix my dress and swipe my fingers under my eyes, hoping my mascara didn't smudge too much, just in time for the door to come flying open. A man and woman I don't recognize come stumbling in, laughter bubbling up when they notice my startled reaction. Pulling myself together, I smile and laugh with them, excusing myself to leave them to their own devices.

Back in the main part of the house, I find Shelby, Lucy, Nathan, and Bryan all enjoying a good laugh, over some story Bryan just told about his latest conquest from last night.

"Where were you?" Shelby asks me.

"I was in the ladies' room."

"Well, you're back, and this party is becoming one hell of a rager and less of a Derby party." She points out.

I look around and notice that it is quite odd that the party has quickly shifted from snobby polite to booze-infused chaos.

"Have you seen Kenny?" I ask anyone who wants to answer, except I get nothing but a bunch of "nos".

After another half hour or so, I decide I'm done for the night. Kenny's actions have thrown me off my game, and I'm feeling oddly vulnerable. Leaning closer to Shelby, I say, "I think I'm going to call it a night." Nodding her head, she offers to leave with me, which I accept before we say our goodbyes to Lucy, Bryan and Nathan. Ivy isn't anywhere to be found, so my friends promise to express my thanks to her for the fun.

Ivy's body fits nicely in the trunk of my candy apple red sports coupe; careful not to get her gorgeous brown hair caught in the lock, I place it gently over her face before closing the trunk door with a thud. I make my way around to the front of the car when I see Harper Ward Lewis-Sheridan and Shelby Barnett-Bowman leaving Ivy's party through the front door. They quickly climb into the back of Harper's waiting SUV, the chauffer closing the door behind them. They don't see me... I lift my hand to my mouth and lick the dried cum from between my fingers. Harper's pussy has a musky scent that drives my senses wild. Her cum tastes like a watermelon on a hot summer's day.

Chapter Thirteen
Nathan

Tonight's party, is sure to be an entirely different affair than last night's.

I can't believe Ivy's party went from a classy affair to a college frat party as quickly as it did. The reports in this morning's paper painted it as a metaphorical bad hair day for Ivy Stallwerth. Although they did manage to get the picture of Ivy, Harper, and Shelby, on the front page with a glowing report on how both the bourbon and horse heiresses made a quiet and discreet departure before the antics of the other guests got to be too much. It was like one of those school dances where the cool kids spike the punch, and everyone gets tipsy from it. I woke up with the worst headache, and I had only had two drinks before attempting to find Ivy and then ultimately leaving soon after Harper and Shelby.

Coming home last night to an empty house was miserable. Maybe it's time to talk to Shelby about helping her out with the Farm and maybe moving back into the house. Maybe it's way too early for that convo. The more I think about it, the more I'm sure it's definitely way too early for that convo.

Turning onto the drive that leads up to the Lewis-Sheridan estate, I take note of the way the grounds, house, stables, all of it are lit up like a Christmas tree on Christmas Eve. It's incredible the way everything glows golden, getting brighter and more defined the closer you get. Evenly spaced oak trees are wrapped in twinkling lights every few feet down both sides of the paved road that is lined by a wooden fence to keep the horses out of harm's way. At the top of the drive, there is a short line of cars waiting their turn for a valet to whisk their chariot away so they can enter the most exquisite home in Kentucky, literally. Not only Home and Garden Magazine, but Architectural Digest and Southern Living all did feature stories on this place and the enigmatic family that lives within its walls. I know because I read them all when I was doing my research before coming out here from the west coast. It is hailed as the most expensive home in the state and boasts one of the most exclusive stable set-ups for a private residence, second only to Bowman Farm. Then what did you expect from the world's oldest Bourbon dynasty? "Enjoy your evening Mr Barnett."

"Thank you," I respond to the young woman taking names at the door and cross-referencing them with her list. The giant bodyguard behind her stands ready to deal with any unwanted interlopers, including the press. No doubt Mrs Ward Lewis-Sheridan will release approved images in the days to follow this exclusive soiree, everyone vying to be in the selected images. It's disgusting, really, comical at best.

The home is, admittedly, magnificent not only in size but interior style.

I find myself wondering if the lady of the house hired a designer or did it all herself. I make my way through the grand, marble-floored foyer, stepping around people dressed to the nines, looking for Harper, Shelby, or both. I pass the Kentucky State Governor and his wife talking to the Louisville Mayor, whose wife is talking to George Clooney and his wife, or is that a date…

Turning the corner into the next room, I find Harper. She is standing with her father, two other men, and one woman. She looks incredible in her gown. It resembles a suit in the way the long-sleeved collard white dress shirt tucks into her light blue ball gown style skirt. She has a thick teal-colored belt wrapped around her waist and a matching fastener on her head. All of the women are wearing them. It wouldn't be an official Derby without them. Harper notices me out of the corner of her eye and motions for me to go over to where she is.

Excusing herself from her conversation, she says, "Nathan. I'm glad you could make it. Is Shelby by chance with you?"

"No, she isn't. I figured she would be here already."

"I'm sure she is on her way. She hates these things, and after last night's party, if you could even call it that, she probably isn't driving too quickly to get here."

"Right. That was a bit of a shit show last night."

"That's one way to look at it, and speaking of… No Ivy tonight?"

"No. I tried calling her earlier but had to leave a message. Besides, I didn't think the invite extended to her." At least I hoped it didn't. It was time to start distancing myself from her to pursue other more attractive and serious matches.

"Smart man." She says this as she signals for a waiter to bring his tray of drinks over. "Drink?" She asks as she grabs one for herself and hands me one.

"Don't mind if I do." It's a bourbon, of course. There are trays of all sorts of stuff floating around, champagne, hors d'oeuvres, charcuterie, and fruit with wine. They thought of everything.

"Come on. I want to show you something." Harper begins to walk towards the open doors to the terrace when her mother cuts us off.

"Harper, darling, who is your friend?"

"Mom, this is Nathan Barnett. Nathan, this is my Mother Elle Lewis Ward-Sheridan."

"Well, Mr Barnett, it is a pleasure to meet you. You wouldn't by chance be related to…" The wheels are turning in that pretty little head of hers, "No, surely not. I apolo…"

"Actually, I am." She didn't have a chance to voice her full question, but I knew she was asking if I was Shelby's runaway brother. No need to continue the lie. "I returned to town a couple of weeks ago after spending a lot of my life to date on the west coast."

"Well, now, that seems like a fascinating story, and I hope that one day very soon, we can chat about it?"

Whether she was genuinely interested or just being nice didn't matter; any chance to be in the same general vicinity of Harper was quickly becoming my main goal. "Absolutely, whenever you want."

"That's just perfect. I hope you are enjoying yourself? I see Harper has already gotten you into the bourbon." She says with a light laugh.

"My mom seems to think that I encourage everyone to drink the bourbon, but may I remind you, Mom, that you are the one who planned the menu." It's said with a light teasing manner, and the two women share a knowing look, and we all have a good laugh over it before her mother excuses herself to mingle with some more of her guests. "Come on." Harper takes my hand in hers and leads us out onto the brick terrace. More people mill about while we pass them, taking a few steps down to the lower portion of the terrace that is all grass, with a huge rectangular pool in the center. Cement pavers are spaced out with grass between them, so we step from paver to paver, making our way around the pool, past the oversized outdoor furniture and lounge chairs that have party-goers relaxing, sipping their cocktails, eating their food, and just enjoying the overall beautiful evening.

Now directly across from the house, Harper continues to step from paver to paver until we run out of pavers, and it's just grass. Stopping briefly, she kicks off her nude-colored heels and leaves them there while leading me to a large tree several feet away. It's one of those trees that has drippy branches and leaves that provide an almost curtain-like façade for whoever is under the tree. Harper releases my hand and extends her arm to part the strands of leaves before walking into the shadowed area. I follow her.

Under the tree, there is a wooden bench swing suspended above the ground from a huge branch several feet above it. Taking my cues from her, I sit next to her on the bench, and we start to swing slowly back and forth. Neither one of us says anything for a few minutes; we just sit there in our comfortable silence until she speaks first.

"I love this little spot."

"It's nice."

"It's where I come when I want to escape my own thoughts. In the morning, the sun streams through the branches. When I was a little girl, I used to pretend the rays of the sun were from a disco ball high up in the tree."

"It sounds magical."

"Not as magical as the summer nights out here when the fireflies dance around your head like little fairies turning you

104

into the belle of the ball."

"Well, they did a fantastic job tonight." As I say it, she turns to look at me, her lips slightly parted and wet from her last sip of bourbon.

"Are you flirting with me, Mr Barnett?"

"Yes. Is that okay with you, Ms Ward Lewis-Sheridan?"

"Only if you promise to kiss me before I change my mind."

"Done." With that, I take her face in both of my hands and kiss the shit out of her. I start gently, but it is quickly evident that I can't control myself, and the kiss turns into something more. It becomes desperate and almost bruising, and she is sucking it up just as much as I am. Before I can think better of it, I pull her to me, and she straddles my lap; it's all over from there when the deep V-neck of her shirt puts her breasts front and center. The curve and creamy color call my name, and I find myself leaving her lips to nip and suckle at her perfect handful-sized tits. They are warm, luscious, and the nipples perk into hard little nubs I can play with, rolling them between my teeth. Harper's hands are in my hair, her nails scraping against my scalp while she tries to keep her audible pleasure from escaping our curtained hideout.

Breathless, she says, "Stop... wait... just... Oh god."

"What is it? Why am I stopping?" I have a raging hard-on, which I know she can feel pressing against her pussy even with my pants and her dress between us. Her breathing is rapid, and she is looking at me like she is trying to figure out the most complicated math problem of her life. "Fuck Harper... If we are going to stop now, then you need t..." I cut off my words when she plants her lips roughly against mine, and her hands start digging at her dress to get it out of the way. *Oh, fuck yes!*

Her hands meet their mark when she pulls my fly down, and her soft, thin fingers wrap around the girth of my cock. At first, I'm thinking she's going to jerk me off, and I'm fully prepared to let her. Fuck that shit. Knowing she will be walking around with my cum all over her thighs for the rest of the night, nearly brings me to orgasm until I realize she is repositioning herself just before she slams herself down on my rock-hard dick.

FUUUCCKKK... The word comes out as an audible groan against her mouth while she begins to move up and down forward and back, giving a little twist here and there. Her pussy feels amazing. Warm, soft, and tight around my monster-sized cock. I grip her hips and help her move this way and that way fucking my brains out, literally. I'm numb all over from this woman's touch, she has the power here, and I'm absolutely fucking willing to let her have at it.

It's only another few strokes before the two of us are coming in unison, her body going limp against mine.

Harper doesn't move for a few minutes while she lets her forehead rest against mine; our mingled breath smells of bourbon and sex; it's the headiest of scents, and I want more. Pressing my hips up, I push my cock deeper into her pussy, her breath catches, but I keep going. My cock is still hard and ready to fuck. There's no way I'm wasting this opportunity. Clearly, neither is she judging by the way her hands grip the strands of my hair while I grip her ass and move from the bench swing to press her back against the rough bark of the tree trunk. Her legs are wrapped around my waist while I plunge my dick into her harder and farther with each stroke. She bites into my shoulder to keep from screaming out loud, it fucking hurts, but it makes me go harder until once again we cum all over one another before I drop us to the ground where our bodies separate and we each fall to our back on the grass and leaf-covered ground. *Holy shit...*

Before I can ask her if she's good, I feel my phone buzz in the back pocket of my black Brioni tuxedo pants. Clearly, I was out of my head when I see seven missed calls and voice mails and eighteen text messages from Shelby. "Something's wrong."

"Yeah, we just fucked in the back yard of my parent's house."

"No, with Shelby," I say it while standing up to tuck my now limp dick back into my pants.

"What do you mean?" She asks, sitting up and adjusting her skirt at the same time.

Reaching out my hand, I help Harper off the ground, and while I watch her fix her shirt and further adjust her skirt, I say, "She left me a bunch of voicemails and a shit ton of text messages saying that she needs to speak to me and its an emergency. She even used shouty capitals."

Pulling her phone out of a pocket in her skirt that I didn't even know existed, she confirms that she has the same on hers just before her face goes white, and she says, "We need to go. Now."

Chapter Fourteen
Shelby

Ugh, I hate getting dressed up for parties. Why did I agree to go to this thing again? Oh yeah, they are like… they are the family I never had but always wished for. The Lewis Ward-Sheridan family has been there for me more times than I can count since Harper and I found out that we are sisters from different mothers, and I suspect many times before that as well.

Walking down the front steps towards my Blue Audi Q7 45 TFSI Quattro Tiptronic, I try my hardest not to trip on the skirt of my Light Green Carolina Herrera Silk organza ball gown. I actually like this one more than I'm willing to admit. When I called her people asking for something to match a fascinator I found and fell in love with, she accepted the challenge and came up with this whimsical and dreamy one-shouldered number that fits like a glove. I just need to remember that I'm walking in heels, not muck boots.

Once I get to the SUV, I throw my matching green clutch on the passenger seat before gathering the skirt of my dress to get in the driver's seat.

I'm glad I went for the roomy model, and had it detailed the other day after getting mud all over the floor mat.

Turning the curve at the top of the driveway, I head down towards the heavy wrought iron gates that have a huge letter "B" in fancy script emblazoned in the middle of each half. I'm only about a third of the way there when I see what looks like a van driving away from the main birthing stable in section "A" of the facility. No one is working in that part of the facility tonight because all of the mares and stud horses are in section "B". Maybe it's a delivery? I don't recall seeing one on the security roster.

Pressing the auto-dial button numbered "one" on my in-dash navigation system, the phone only rings twice before John answers and checks the roster for deliveries. He tells me that a driver for Chester's grain and feed dropped off a load of feed in facility "C", and that they were, in fact, in a white van that just pulled out onto the main road.

After thanking John for the information, I send a voice dictated text to Harper to let her know I'm running late, and head towards facility "A". We don't use Chester's for feed; the last delivery we accepted from them was five years ago. Something isn't right, and when I pull up in front of the stables, a pit forms in the bottom of my stomach. Maybe I should call John back and have him meet me here before I just go barging into find who-knows-what in there. Hopefully, it's nothing; hopefully, it was a simple mistake that can be cleared up in the morning.

I decide to stop being a baby and just open the door to check it out. It's practically pitch-black inside, with very little light from the auxiliary safety lighting. Lifting my skirt to keep from getting dirt and hay from the floor on it, I make my way to the panel on the wall that has all of the lighting and power controls for this stable and the stalls within it. Flipping them all on, I turn around and stop dead in my tracks. Hanging from the ceiling halfway down the walkway, suspended from both wrists, is Ivy Stallwerth's naked and scalped dead body. For the second time in a handful of days, I find myself running for the nearest bucket I forget all about my gorgeous green dress as I fall to my knees and puke up everything I have consumed today.

When I find my way back outside to my Audi, I contemplate the irony of Ivy's dead body being dumped on my doorstep. I seem to have become a halfway house for the murdered. Logically I know I should call the police, but I find myself calling and failing several times to get a hold of Nate and Harper, who are at the same party I'm supposed to be at right at this very moment.

Blessedly after an hour of sitting here hoping nobody comes to check on what I'm doing, Nate's Blacked out Range Rover comes into view.

"What the hell happened?" He asks as soon as he's out of the driver's seat.

"How the hell am I supposed to know! I saw a van leaving and came up here to check it out only to find that…" I finish pointing at the closed door to the stable.

"Have you called the police yet?" Harper asks.

"No. But I definitely need to. We can't bury this one out back with Tom." The gravity of our precarious situation is not lost on any of us. Neither, for me, is the fact that Harper's hair is disheveled and the skirt of her dress is very wrinkled. Come to think of it, Nate's normally very neat hair is also disheveled. "OH MY GOD! You two had sex, didn't you! That's why it took so fucking long for you to answer me!"

"Shelby, please…" Harper starts to deny it, but I give her that knowing look that dares her to lie to me. "OKAY FINE! We did have sex. Happy?"

"Am I happy that you were fucking my brother while I

was finding his dead girlfriend…"

"Actually, she's not my girlfr…"

"DOES IT MATTER! For fucks sake! There's a dead woman in my stable!"

"You're right," Harper says it quietly. "I'm sorry you had to wait so long for us to get here." When she finishes that last part, she moves towards the door before I stop her with a hand on her arm.

"No, Harper. You don't want to go in there. It's terrible, and we don't want to mess anything up for when the police get here." Lifting my cell to my ear, I place the call we are all hoping doesn't come back to bite us in the ass.

While we wait for the police to get here, we get our stories straight; thankfully, John, one of my trusted security guys, agrees to back our story.

Logically he knows Harper and Nate just got here, and I was at the house when the white van arrived and then again left the property, so it was an easy favor to ask when he joined us at the stable to wait for the police.

Officer Gaines is the first to arrive; sirens can be heard in the distance signaling the arrival of more officers and hopefully someone to take Ivy's body out of the stable.

"I didn't think I would be seeing you so soon, ladies and…?" Officer Gaines is speaking to Harper and me but looking at Nate.

"Nathan Barnett." He answers her.

"And this is John, one of the security guards here at the Farm," I say, motioning in John's direction. "He is one of the guards on duty tonight."

Disregarding my introduction to John, Officer Gaines asks, "Any relation to one another?" Blessedly before either

111

Nate or I can answer, the other officers pull up and start asking her questions, prompting her to head over to the stable doors, but not before she has a chance to say, "I'm not done with you four. I suggest you get comfortable."

It's several hours before the police leave my property. Officer Gaines and two other detectives are still here, though. She wants to question us and has made it clear that it either has to happen here or at the station. None of us wants to go to the station, so we agree to move the party to my office two buildings over. It's comfortable enough for this particular purpose but a little small for all of the bodies considering all three of us now have our lawyers present. After some thought, Officer Gaines agrees to take John's statement first, accompanied by my lawyer, so that he can get home to his family, and we move locations to my private residence. Harper's parents have also come to support both Harper and me. I'm grateful that they didn't have to leave in the middle of their party as we decided to call them somewhere around two o'clock in the morning.

Harper changed into a pair of my yoga pants and an oversized hoodie, while I changed into my usual jeans and long-sleeved Henley. Nate stayed in his own clothes but opted to fix his hair a bit.

One at a time, Officer Gaines takes us into a separate room for questioning. Apparently, because it's my house, I have to go last or some lame shit like that. Everyone stays anyhow to make sure I'm okay. It's humbling how truly loved I am by these people, including the brother I haven't seen in almost twelve years.

"So tell me what happened tonight?" Officer Gaines asks.

She sits across the table from me with her little notebook and tape recorder, ready to note everything I say.

"What exactly do you want to know?"

"Everything. Start at the beginning."

So I do. I talk about stressing over almost tripping on my dress because of how much I actually like this one, and my not looking forward to going to the party but wanting to support my family. I mention my observations about the van while Harper, Nathan, and I attempt to leave the house.

"Tell me something," She says, "Why did Nathan and Harper leave the party to come to see you here if you were going there?"

Thankfully we had all agreed on an answer to this question before her earlier arrival. "It's stupid really, but I needed help with my makeup and hair, and I really didn't want to show up at her house half done up. You know?"

"I see. So you guys were driving back to Harper's when you spotted the van?"

"Yes. That's when I called John to ask about the delivery log."

"And you were all in the same car?"

"No. I was in mine with Harper, and Nathan was behind us in his."

"Tell me about Mr Barnett. I never got the answer to my earlier question about yours and his connection."

"I'm sure you're aware that after my father died, my older brother ran away?"

"I am."

"Well, that's him. Nathan is my brother. He came back a couple of weeks ago."

"Just out of the blue? Your long-lost brother shows up. His

113

girlfriend ends up dead while he's coincidentally at a party with another woman. That doesn't seem weird to you?"

Well, when you put it that way. "Ivy wasn't Nate's girlfriend. And he wasn't at a party with another woman. He was at a party, but it was at the invitation of Lincoln Ward-Sheridan since he is a potential business associate. Harper just so happens to live there and work with her father."

"I was under the assumption that he and Ivy were an item since they have been seen around town together quite often lately."

"You assumed incorrectly. Add to that, that Harper is my best friend and Nate is my brother. Why wouldn't they come help me together?"

Officer Gaines mulls that over for a moment before asking me to tell her more about Nate and his whereabouts, according to what I know. She also asks about Ivy's party, if I noticed anything odd or out of the ordinary. I'm shocked to learn that Ivy has been dead for almost twenty-four hours, and her party planner had reported her missing just after her party cleared out. I guess she went looking around the house for her to get her final payment for services rendered and couldn't find her anywhere. It may have been an overreaction, but the planner called the police to file a report when they told her there was nothing they could legally do for her at that point. I wonder if Nate knew that she's been missing since before her party ended. I can't even think back to when at her party I saw her last. I do end up telling Officer Gaines about the odd way the party went from respectful to crazy weird in a short time frame. I don't think it seems weird to her, but it definitely wasn't normal.

After another two hours of questions, follow-up

questions, and more questions for all of us, Officer Gaines finally leaves and takes her friends with her, but not before making us all agree to come by the station later that day to finalize, and sign our typed-up statements. And to also assign an officer to keep watch. Just in case. By this point, it's already after eight o'clock in the morning, and we are all exhausted.

The lawyers have left, and Harper only agrees to go home with her parents because Nate promises to stay here with me instead of going home.

It's like I'm some fragile child that needs looking after, although, if I'm being honest with myself, I'm glad that at least one of them is going to stay here. The thought that a serial killer is running loose with a penchant for killing brunettes, and can clearly access my property is freaking me out more than I let on to the others.

Chapter Fifteen
Shelby

Waking up, I look over at the clock on my bedside table. It reads three o'clock in the afternoon. How did I sleep for a solid six hours and already feel like I need a nap? I suppose there's no use hoping that last night was nothing but a bad dream. I sit up. The sheets and blankets I had fallen asleep with are a huge mess. Twisted this way and that. My sleep shorts are crooked, and my t-shirt is damp from sweat. Belatedly I can feel the pounding in my head, which gets worse the more I move. Lovely. I slept like shit, and I have a migraine.

Hopefully, that goes away before I have to go and sit in a windowless room at the police station with Officer Gaines; otherwise, this day is going to suck almost as much as last night.

The hot steamy shower that I spent nearly an hour in did nothing to quell my aching head or body, and I just didn't feel like wearing my usual jeans, so after sliding on a pair of leggings and an oversized sweater, I attempt to make my way downstairs before I remember that Nate slept here last night. It was so spur of the moment I didn't have to wonder if he would want to stay in his old room or not, so I showed him to one of the numerous guest rooms down the hallway from my own room. Once the dust had settled after my mother died, my first priority was to renovate the inside of this house. The first

floor stayed pretty much the same structurally; however, all of the rooms were remodeled with new paint, furniture and all of the old stuff was either donated or burned. Most of it was burned. The second and third floors were completely renovated and remodeled. Some of the rooms were combined to form larger rooms, others were converted for other purposes than their original, and the attic… half of it was boarded up, and the other half was only left open and available for safety and maintenance purposes. The only rooms left untouched were my dad's personal office and attached study, and Nate's childhood bedroom. I frequently thought better about my decision to only board off the part of the attic that served as my living space for so long, but in the end decided that I liked having that reminder of where I came from, where today's Shelby was curated. It's no wonder I regularly see a therapist.

Knocking on the guestroom door where I left Nate earlier this morning, it pushes open on its own to reveal an empty room. Maybe he is downstairs.

Making my way farther down the hall to the back stairwell, I notice that the door to his childhood bedroom is slightly ajar. Quietly approaching the opening, I peek through and see Nate standing in front of one of the huge windows that look out at the open expanse of pastures behind the house. His back is to the door, and he is still wearing his tuxedo pants and shirt from last night. At the foot of the bed, his shoes are placed side by side, and his suit jacket is folded neatly on the end of the bed. As he is standing there looking across the property towards where we were reacquainted only a couple of nights ago, I wonder what he is thinking about.

His hands are in his pants pockets, and his hair, I notice, is damp from an earlier shower. For so many years, I had resigned myself to the idea that my older brother was dead. That the Nate I knew as a young girl was no longer out in the world waiting to come home, except he was, and he did, but he most definitely isn't the Nate I knew as a child. This man before me has had to do so many things on his own; I suppose we are alike in that way. What must it have been like for him? Did he love his adopted mom more than his real family? He must have hated us. Maybe that's why it took him so long to come home.

"The view hasn't changed since the last time I stood here looking at it."

I didn't realize he knew I was standing there. "I'm sorry, I didn't mean to spy on you."

"It's your house. You can do what you please. I should apologize for snooping around."

Is he serious? "Um, this is just as much your home as it is mine. Please don't apologize for looking around."

"But is it really?" At those words, he turns around to look at me, now standing just inside the door. "I left twenty-two years ago and never bothered to reach out once to let you know I was still alive. And that I thought about you every single day of those twenty-two years."

I don't know what to say to him, so I opt for the truth. "I thought about you too. Every day. I was so mad at you for so long because you didn't just leave this house, you left me, and when I was done being mad at you, it was easier for me to pretend that you had died rather than think about you living life out in the world without me."

He had been looking at his bare feet while I spoke, but when he looks at me now, I see the glistening tears of his Shame? Regret? Sadness? And then he says, "I'm sorry,

Shelby. I should have been here for you when you needed me. If I had been here..." His words cut off in a choked cry. I've never seen a grown man cry before. I do the only thing I know how to do and hug him. I hug him tight, and he hugs me in return. Then I cry, and we cry together. We cry for all of the memories we have together, the memories we have alone, the memories we will make, the time we have lost, and the time we will have together.

"I'm sorry to Nate. For everything." It's a little bit before we are both calmed enough to have a conversation without shedding any more tears. We talk about what sort of things he did when he was growing up on the west coast and about how much I would love Seattle. I tell him about everything I did with the business and the house in more detail than the other night. And then we talk about Harper and me and the circumstances behind our birth, our relationship, and his feelings for her. That last part prompts me to tell him that I'm sorry for what happened to Ivy, whose death doesn't impact him as emotionally as it might another man. Turns out that he didn't know her as closely as we all thought he did. In fact, he tells me that he barely knew her outside of their limited interactions, which amounted to two or three dates and one sleepover. "Ew, Nate. You slept with Ivy? I wouldn't tell Harper that. Especially since you slept with her last night." I want to laugh at the situation of my brother and me talking about his sexual conquests, one of which I found dead last night.

"Please. It's not like Harper hasn't had sex with other men before last night."

At this point in our conversation, we have grabbed some food from the subzero fridge in my kitchen, stopped at his house so he could change, and are now headed to the police station to see Officer Gaines. I texted Harper to let her know, and she said she would meet us there. "True, but man, you and Harper. So how is that going to look?"

"What do you mean?"

"I mean, are you in love with her, just looking to keep having sex, want to put a ring on it?"

"Why don't we slow down a little bit there." He laughs as he says it, and I reach over to punch him in the arm. See... It's like we never missed a beat.

Nate sits in another room, I presume, while I'm here in this room with Officer Gaines. It's almost as small as a shoebox. No windows except for the one two-way mirror on the wall across from me. I wonder how many people are standing behind it watching me? Is it just me, or is it chilly in here? Do they do that on purpose?

"... that Ivy was missing for much of her party the other night, is that correct? Shelby..."

"I'm sorry, what?" Shit... I need to focus.

"I was asking you if it was correct that Ivy was missing for much of her party the other night."

"Yes. That's correct, although I don't know for how long exactly. There were a lot of people there, and since she was the hostess, I didn't think it was too unusual at the time."

"It didn't seem odd to you that your brother wasn't with her instead of hanging out with you and your friends?"

"Not at all..." I mean, it did at the time, but now that I know how it really was... "Like I told you last night, they weren't dating and hardly knew one another."

Officer Gaines sits across from me, nothing but a manila

folder in front of her on the table. They record the conversations in this room on a device in the adjoining room. She's just watching me; it makes me nervous, though I try not to show it. After what seems like an hour, she says, "Why do you think the killer left Ivy's body in your stable?"

"I have no idea. I could ask you the same question, I suppose."

"You could." Tapping her fingertips on the manila envelope, almost like she's debating showing me what's in it or not, she says, "My theory is that whoever is targeting these brunette women, scalping them and dumping their bodies in places to be found, is connected to Bowman Fa..."

"I'm sorry?" That is not what I expected her to say at all when I cut her off, appalled that she would suggest such a thing... "We have a rigorous background and security check on all of our employees. As you know, we cater our services to people who have a lot of money and require a lot of discretion and protection with regards to their horses."

"I have no doubts about that."

"Then why do you..." I stop talking when she pulls a series of photos out of her folder and slides them across the table to now lie in front of me. The picture on top is of Ivy's dead body lying on a morgue table. Covering my mouth with my hand to stop my gagging, I also squeeze my eyes shut.

Officer Gaines reaches over and fans the photos out. My sick curiosity gets the better of me, but I still ask her, "Why are you showing me these?" Tears form in my eyes.

She taps on one photo and says, "Just like the others, Ivy is missing her scalp of brown hair."

"That doesn't mean that..."

"And in this one, she is missing a patch of skin. Again,

121

just like the others…"

"How does this mean that someone from Bowman Farm did this?"

Ignoring my question, she continues to point at the pictures and says, "And just like the others, when we did an infrared scan of the muscle and tissues in the area of the missing skin, we found this…" She now points to the final picture in the group waiting for me to look at it.

I don't want to look, but I do. It takes a minute for me to recognize the letter that was obviously carved into her skin and that of the other women. On the page is a compilation of different body parts, all with a missing section of skin and all depicting the same letter "B" in elegant script. An exact duplicate of the one anyone who enters or leaves the private area of Bowman Farm sees on the Gate at the end of my driveway. *Fuck my life*

"And I don't recall saying that someone at Bowman Farm was responsible, Ms Barnett-Bowman."

"Then who do yo…" Dawn breaks on marble head. "Oh my god! You think I did this?" I'm definitely going to be sick again. How could… That's a stupid question; she knows what I did to my mother and possibly uncle.

"Did you do this?"

"NO!" I push the pictures back towards her and vehemently deny any and all connection to these murders. "I did not kill any of these women, and I have no idea who did."

"It doesn't seem odd to you that they are all brunettes. Like yourself. And that they all have the same letter as your last name carved into their flesh, which is missing and assumed to be a trophy along with their scalps of brown hair?"

"Oh, it seems odd and disgusting, and disturbing for sure.

But I swear to you that I had nothing to do with any of this."

"I know you didn't."

Are you fucking kidding me right now? "Then why are you interrogating me like you think I did?"

"Because I think you may know the person who did this. I think that person is closer to you than you know."

"Who... no. You think that Nathan did this?"

"Possibly. His return to Louisville coincides with the timeframe for the first murder, and he has a sordid history. Sometimes people with tragic pasts do things in their future to try and make it right."

"So you think my brother returned from the west coast to murder brown-haired women and then carved the initial of our last name into their skin, kept it and their hair?" This is insane, "For what reason?"

"Your mother was a brunette, wasn't she?"

"Your point?"

"Possibly, this is his way of getting his anger for her out of his system. He can't torture and kill her," She gives me a pointed look that says, *Since you already killed her.* Before she continues to say, "So he finds women who resemble her in their hair color and makes them pay for her sins against him."

There isn't much for her to ask me after that revelation, so I am released from the interrogation room after I sign my statement and consult with my lawyer, who remained mostly silent at my request since I have nothing to hide. Harper is being escorted into her own interrogation room with her lawyer just as we are walking into the hallway. Strategic moves for sure. I ask the on-duty officer at the reception window in the lobby where Nathan is when I don't see him waiting. It turns out he is already in his own little windowless interrogation room and left a message for me not to wait for him. That he will call me when he's done. Is he really anticipating being here that long? Is it possible that Officer Gaines is right? I mean, I really don't know anything about the man who I haven't seen in twenty-two years. That's a long time and plenty of time for someone to change. If anyone knows what our mother's toxic lies could do to a person, it's definitely me.

When I get into the driver's seat of my Audi, I decide right then and there that if Nate is responsible for these murders, I will do everything in my power to help him through the legal proceedings and get him the help that he needs for himself. There is no question that I will stand by his side and help him through it all.

As soon as I got home from the police station, I went straight to my private office and started doing my own research on the murders, Nathan and his company. Reasoning it out to myself, I just wanted to have some perspective. See if there was anything that made sense to me about anything in regards to all of it.

I started with Nathan and his life in Seattle. I figured if there was anything suspicious, then I could ask about it before the police just threw it out there. Page after page of information on the mysterious man named Nathan Lincoln Barnett came up on my screen; about his upbringing at the hands of a woman he once tried to mug, starting his own business as an impressionable teenager, inheriting everything after his adopted mom passed away. All things I already knew, and then it came up, staring right at me from my computer screen was the face of a woman I recognized except in this photo and all the others I found, she was younger and a lot less put together than she is today or even was the other night. Kendal, or as she was called then, Kendra had brown hair, and when she was twelve, her parents died in a house fire. Kendra was the only survivor.

After bouncing from home to home, the woman who "adopted" Nate also "adopted" Kendra from right off the streets after she ran away from what would be her last placement home. There were a few articles ridiculing Nate for not taking his "sister" in after their adopted mom died. And for not sharing the inheritance he received with her, instead leaving her to fend for herself.

How long has Kendal or Kendra... Lived here? She and Harper have been friends for a couple of years, maybe? It doesn't make sense. If Kendal is this Kendra person, why hasn't she said anything to anyone, let alone Nate? Does Nate even know that she is here? And then it hits me. Officer Gaines said that people have a way of getting their anger for others out in some pretty sick ways. What if Kendal is the murderer and is trying to frame Nate for it? Does Officer Gaines know... I grab my cell off the mahogany and glass desk, dialing Nate's cell number, but it goes right to voicemail. "Nate, it's Shelby. You need to call me as soon as you get this. I think I know who is committing the murders." Halfway down the front stairs of the house, I stop to debate my next call...

Harper or Officer Gaines, Harper it is, except just like my last call, it goes to voicemail this time after several rings. "Harper, you need to call me as soon as you can. I know who killed those women, and it wasn't Nate. Also, stay away from..." Now at the bottom of the stairs, I hear a noise come from the kitchen, so I finish my message with, "Just call me.

Please hurry."

I put my phone in the pocket on the side of my leggings and think twice about going to see what that noise was or just leaving and calling Officer Gaines from the car. I decide on the latter and turn towards the double front doors when something slams into the back of my head, sending my world spinning before it goes black.

Chapter Sixteen
Nathan

Un-fucking real. They actually think I committed all those murders.

Thank fuck I have a fantastic attorney, and they had zero hard evidence, only theories and speculation. Finally, after more than hours than it should have taken, I am walking out of the hallway where the interrogation rooms are and into the lobby when I see Harper talking to her lawyer and another man dressed similarly, probably a second attorney. Is it possible that she has been here this long as well? I can't understand why. After all, it's me they think did it.

Looking over her shoulder Harper dismisses the two men and walks over to me. "How did it go?"

"Yours probably went better," I respond and think about the one question, among the hundreds that disturbed me more than any of the ones before or even after it. Office Gaines asked about my relationship with my mother before I left home. She read in the initial missing persons' report after I ran away that my mother and I were very close. Always spending time together. My only answer was to say that I was a young boy. She was my mother. What else would be going on? That's when Officer Gaines saw right through me. She hit the nail on the head when she concluded that my mother had sexually abused me the night my father died, and then again, the night

I ran away. Apparently, not only was she a lying psychopathic bitch, but she was a rapist. It's no longer a mystery to me as to why she would sleep with my uncle, or rather my father. How did Lincoln not see it in either one of them? And then she asked about Kendra.

"They must not think you did it any more. Since you're standing here and all."

Harper doesn't sound like the Harper I have come to know outside of the boardroom. She sounds very business-like and, matter of fact. "They have nothing but theories and speculation. NO actual evidence to say that I did any of it."

"We didn't use protection last night when we fucked."

Ah. There's the reason for her current tone. "I know. We were a little out of control last night and didn't have time to think about it."

"You came inside of me twice."

What is she playing at with this? I look around to see if anyone is listening or close enough to hear and say, "I'm sorry, Harper, but it..."

She cuts me off and says, "I'm not looking for an apology, Nathan. I just had to say it out loud. It's been on my mind since it happened. It's not like me to allow that to happen, but... you..." she takes a resigned sigh and laughs softly before finishing with, "You are dangerous for me."

"Right back at you, gorgeous." I return her smile and ask, "Have you talked to Shelby, at all?"

"No. After texting her to tell her I would meet you guys here, I jumped in the shower before leaving. You guys were already in a room when I arrived.

Strategically, I'm sure; they made me sit out here and wait until they were finished with Shelby. They actually walked me into a room just as she was walking out of another one. As if we were going to scare into a confession of some sort. Idiots"

"That's probably why they let us leave at the same time. I can't imagine they had a lot to ask you." It wasn't exactly a question, but it was in the sense that I was curious what they asked her, or even more so, what they told her.

"I'm sure, but in any case, let's go. I want to go find Shelby, and make sure she's all right."

"Right. My car is at m…"

"It's a good thing I have mine then." She says it as a joke, but yes, later, it would unknowingly turn out to be a very big thing for me.

The drive to Shelby's house only takes about an hour. That's the drawback to her living on the farm. The amount of space it needs far exceeds what the city limits can hold, although Harper lives about the same distance in the other direction, so she's used to it. Me on the other hand, I feel like we should talk, but I'm also finding the silence between us to be comfortable. At one point, Harper was driving the speed limit until she noticed the voicemail icon on her in-dash navigation system. It was from Shelby. Remembering at that point to turn mine back on, I had one as well. Respectively we both listened to them, and now as we pull into the drive leading up to Bowman Farm and Shelby's private residence, Harper is doing over a hundred in this little sports car of hers. As a side note, I can't help but be impressed with not only the way the car takes the dips and curves of the roads but how well Harper commands the vehicle.

Coming to a skidding stop at the guard shack, Harper commands the guard to call the police and direct them to the house before she threatens his life, telling him that if that damn gate isn't open when she gets there, he will live to regret this night. It must have worked because the gate is barely open enough for Harper to navigate her Veyron through it and up the drive without a scratch. Again, she skids to a stop, and we both throw our doors open before running up the front steps to the closed front door.

Instead of rushing into the house, we both abruptly stop at the door, giving one another a look of solidarity Harper reaches out and turns the knob pushing the door open. Causing a loud thud, the door hits the wall adjacent to it. No one comes rushing at us. In fact, the house is quiet, but all of the lights are on. All of the times I observed Shelby in the house, she never turned all of the lights on. Only the ones she needed at the time.

"Nate…"

I look over at Harper, who has her eyes fixed on something ahead of us on the floor. Looking in the general direction of her stare, I see Shelby's cell phone and a smear of blood on the wall just above it. "Don't touch it. We need to find her, come on." Closing the door, we head off in the same direction, looking for my sister. We search room after room making our way through the house.

"The police should be here soon," Harper says this as she pushes the door to Shelby's office open.

There's more of the same in here, nothing. Shelby isn't anywhere to be found in this house. "Why did they take her? I don't understand…"

Standing at Shelby's laptop Harper starts typing on the keys and says, "Oh my god. I think I know what she was going to tell us."

"What?" I ask as I walk over to the other side of the desk.

"Shelby found out that Kendal is the killer. But I just don't understand."

"Who's…" Looking at the picture on the screen, I whisper, "Shit."

"Do you know who that is?"

"It's my sister, well 'adopted' sister from when I lived in Seattle."

"Kendal is your sister?"

"What? No. That's…" Pointing at the picture, I say, "Kendra."

"I'm so confused." Harper runs her hand over her forehead and says, "That girl looks just like my friend, Kendal."

"But that's not possible? Is it?" Fuck me. "Wait. I haven't actually seen or talked to Kendra in months. Amy, my assistant, has talked to her, but how…" Just then, my thought is cut off by Officer Gaines yelling "*HELLO*" at the door downstairs.

Once Officer Gaines has done a bag and tag on Shelby's phone, forensics has finished dusting the entire house and swabbing the blood, taking pictures, looking at security footage, and instructing Harper and me not to leave the front parlor, we are able to finally tell her our theory, the same one Shelby must have come up with. We think that Kendra moved here when she learned about my plans to come here as well. In her jilted state, because of my cutting her out of the money and business, she changed her name, took all of the money I gave her, and used it to set herself up nicely while I thought she was pissing it away.

She was killing brunette women because they resembled

Shelby, my biological sister and the sister I cared about above anything else. Ivy was a brunette that I gave my attention to; no matter how briefly, she had to go. And when Shelby figured it out... She became a liability to Kendra. Or maybe Shelby was just another one of her targets that coincidentally figured it out at the same time.

"I've sent officers to Kendal's residence. If she is a part of this, we will figure it out. In the meantime, you two need to go home and stay there. Understood?"

"No. I can't just wait around here while Shelby could be out there being..." My words choke off, and Harper pulls me into a firm hug.

"Officer Gaines, you don't understand how much Shelby means to both of us. Asking us to just sit here and wait when she's out there needing help..."

Harper begins to cry now, and it's my turn to comfort her.

"I understand, but the two of you running around getting in the..." Her cell phone rings and she steps a few feet away to answer it. "Gaines... uh huh... okay, did you ask the neighbors?" Looking at the two of us standing there watching her with bated breath, she continues, "I see... Thank you. That was the detective I sent to Kendal's house." Clearly thinking about her next words, she says, "It's been burned to the ground."

"What?" Harper says exactly what I'm thinking. "Was she in it?"

"Someone was. But I suspect it wasn't your sister, either of them. Of course, we won't know for sure until we get dental records back from the autopsy. We got lucky time-wise. It seems that the fire was set and put out before my guys arrived. Neighbors said they heard some noises in the apartment, almost like a struggle before they smelled smoke and the whole building went up."

"Oh my god, no one else was hurt, were they?" Harper asks.

"No, but a lot of people lost their homes tonight. I need to go see where we are and find your sisters." With that, Officer Gaines directs a uniformed officer to watch us to ensure we don't leave this room until she says so.

Chapter Seventeen
Shelby & The Cave

"You are too smart for your own good, Shelby."

I can hear her voice, but I can't see her. I try to move my head around to find her, but I can't move anything; my legs, my arms, nothing. Why can't I move? I can't even talk back to her. Oh my god...

"Don't worry, Shelb, you're not going to die just yet. We still have a way to go. And don't worry about your limbs. They are still there, love. I've given you a little dose of Anectine, so you can't move. But you won't sleep either." I know her voice, but my brain is fuzzy. I can't remember what happened. How did I get here? Where is here?

"I'm almost ready to start with you, sister. We are sisters, aren't we?" Just then, Kendal (or is it Kendra?) comes into view. I try with all of my might to move, to grab at her, to fight back against her, but I can't. Nothing is working. "There-there, my sweet sister." With those words, Kendal leans over and licks the tears from my cheeks. She makes a show of savoring the salty wetness on her tongue, and I'm helpless. I can only see as far my vision will let me.

Are those? She has exact copies of my twin chandeliers that are in my dining room. Those are the only things I kept of my mothers, mostly because they weren't even my mothers. When my grandfather had built the house for his first wife, he commissioned them from Tiffany's, had them installed as an anniversary gift, and that's where they have been ever since. Why does she have these copies?

Kendal, still leaning over me, follows my gaze with her own before answering my unspoken question. "We have matching chandeliers, Shelby. Isn't it precious? That's something that you and Harper don't share, isn't it? Let me turn them up for you." Moving away from me, she turns the lights up, and I can see the chandeliers more clearly, as well as the room we are in. Or should I say cavern? We are in a cave built into one of the many limestone hills and rock areas. The light from the crystals bounces around the room and reflects like little twinkles on tiny rocks in the walls whose surface was sheared off when this cave was formed hundreds of years ago.

"So pretty." Why does she have replicas of my chandeliers? It's almost as if she can read my mind when she says, "My mother used to rave on and on about those chandeliers. Well, the ones in your dining room, that is. You see, she would obsess over them all day and gush about them and the two perfect little children she was a nanny for during dinner almost every night until her and my dad died in a house fire." Laughing, she comes back into my view with a hot iron poker in her hand, the tip glowing a bright orange-reddish color. "Now I know what you're thinking. You're thinking that's so tragic and sad that her parents died in a house fire, and let me tell you, it's really not." Please, God, don't let her... "You see, my dad was a good man and my mom a good woman until they started working for your family. In just a matter of a couple of years, they both became avid gamblers at the races.

Taking tips from your dad. When they won, it was fantastic, but when they lost, it wasn't so fun."

How did I not know who Kendal really was? Then I never actually met the nanny's kid. Or even knew she existed since I was only two. Kendal continues to tell me her story, "After too many losses one year, my dad started using drugs and drinking to feel better about himself. He practically gambled away everything we had. They had stopped taking me to the races with them because he was doing drugs in the bathroom and hitting up bookies for more money while my mom was selling herself to the same bookies for extra cash." She's getting mad, I can hear it in her voice, and it's confirmed when she digs her burning hot poker into my leg, or at least I think she does? I still can't feel anything... *Dear God in heaven, please...* "One morning, she showed up at work, and your father fired her. It seems he had heard about their activities after hours at the various tracks around the area and wanted better for his children."

I don't know what is happening. Oh God, why can't I move... "He didn't even give her a severance package. Just showed her the door and called it a day. That night she and my dad went to the track to try and make some scratch. When they got home, I was in bed praying that they weren't someone trying to break in. I had been home alone all day. They began to fight, yelling and screaming at one another. I climbed out of bed and went to see what the loud crash was, and I saw my mom's nose bleeding, and the fighting just kept going. When he followed her into the kitchen, I walked over to his lit cigarette and put it on the carpeted floor under the curtains."

I don't know why she stops talking, but when she says her next words, I wish with every fiber of my being that I could move or at least close my eyes, "There we are..." Kendal holds up what looks like a piece of thick tan-colored fabric with a charred black and red elegant-looking "B" inscribed on it…

"Beautiful, isn't it?" I must be crying. I have to be. It's the only way my body can express the pain and anger, fear and fight… How could someone like her have gone unnoticed this long? I didn't do anything to hurt her. Why is she punishing me?

"There you go again with the tears, Shelby. Really sister, you should stop. But then you're probably wondering why I'm doing this to you, aren't you?" Kendal pauses and looks at me; belatedly, I think I can feel a burning sensation in my leg, but I'm not sure.

"You see, Shelby, you have the adoration of the brother I never had and always wanted. It was a pure coincidence when I ended up in Seattle being adopted by the same woman as Nathan. The social services people here had gone to your mother and asked her if she would be willing to take me in since my mom used to work for her and all. She flat-out refused and sent them away.

I watched from the waiting car when she shut the door in the social worker's face." Kendal is running her hand up my leg and side, or I presume she is.

It's like I feel a shadow of her touch or something. What is going on here…

"From then on, I went from home to home all across the Midwest until I ended up running away from the last home when the dad tried to rape me." She has a faraway look in her eyes for the briefest of moments and then continues to say, "And then I found Nathan and discovered all of his little secrets, and yours.

And then you introduced me to Harper. Unknowingly, of course." Harper… No. Dear God, please don't… Did I just.

"There it is. Your voice is coming back to you. Which means that you're going to start feeling a lot of pain from all over your body. It's a good thing I have already shackled you down. And feel free to scream as loud as you want. No one will hear you." Kendal starts to move away before she stops and says, "Don't worry your pretty little head about Harper. She will never experience this." She waves her hand over my body to demonstrate her example of what Harper will never experience. I pray to God that she means it truthfully. "No... Harper will only suffer from loss at my hands with pleasure closely followed.

Once you are gone, and Nathan follows suit, Harper will look to me for comfort in her time of need. You see, I love her. Harper Adalynn Ward Lewis-Sheridan is my equal in every way."

It takes all of my effort and quickly fleeing strength to fight through the pain that is taking over my body from head to toe. Nothing but pain, however, I manage to squeak out, "to go g-g-good f-f-f-f-for y-y-you."

"I'm sorry, what was that?" Harper leans over me, positioning her ear above my mouth, which is drier than the Sahara. I try my hardest to muster enough strength to repeat it, but Kendal moves away and says, "It was a rhetorical question anyhow, Shelb. I heard it the first time, and I think you're wrong. But then you weren't there when she was coming all over my hand at Ivy's party." She moves to a table off to my left and comes back with a glass full of some sort of clear liquid with bubbles in it. "Since you're starting to feel things again, how about we kick start this process with some fun." Kendal then proceeds to pour the liquid on my head, and when I feel the burn, there is no way I can stop the broken scream that comes out of my mouth. "Would you like to see yourself now, sister?"

Moving the table to an upright position, Kendal then rolls a mirror in front of me. Bile immediately comes up and trickles out of my mouth in waves as I heave and cry and scream at what has been done to me. The piece of skin she removed from my stomach left a huge patch of muscle and tissue bare and bleeding. I'm bleeding from between my legs and can see some abrasions on my inner thighs; there are bruises and cuts all over my body. But the worst part is my missing scalp. My head is nothing but an orb of blood and other bodily fluids. The liquid she poured over my head brought fresh blood streaming down my face over the dried blood that was already there. My body heaves, and more bile comes up, mixing with the blood from my other wounds. "P-p-p-please…" I manage to whisper the word out in hopes that a miracle might happen and she will take it all back. Maybe I'll wake up, and this will all have been a terrible nightmare.

"I'm sorry, Shelby, but it's too late to go back now," Kendal says this as she pushes the table I'm on back into a laying position. My heartbeat is loud in my ears, whooshing in and out… *whoosh, whoosh, whoosh, whoosh*… It's all I can hear. It drowns out my sobs and pleas for mercy. The pain is excruciating, and I beg her to just end this. Blessedly when my world goes black once again, I feel an odd sense of relief that it is my time to meet my maker.

Epilogue
Harper at Bowman Farm

The summer sun is excruciating today, and I want to be at home by the pool; however, I promised Nate that I would check on Stella and give her some love. It's not like there aren't a ton of trainers or stable hands around that could do it, but Stella was Shelby's thoroughbred, and we both want to make sure she doesn't forget that she is loved. Trotting around in the wide-open field, I can feel Stella gearing up to a trot and pull back on her reins. "I know, girl, I'm sorry, but we can't run free today. I promise when we get back to the stables, I'll trot you around the training ring. Okay?" In answer, Stella gives me a neigh, and we head back towards the training area.

It's been three months since Shelby was taken, and there has been no sign of Kendal since the night of Ivy's party. There haven't even been any other murders to offer a clue to the police as to where she might be. Officer Gaines says that she put out a nationwide BOLO but has gotten nothing back. They even brought the FBI in on the case. Facial recognition last picked Kendal up the night of Ivy's party, about an hour before she showed up at my parent's house. She was dropping one of her two cars off on the street across from Ivy's brownstone.

My parents pleaded with me for a week straight after Shelby was taken to move back in with them. I finally conceded to the request but didn't sell the penthouse downtown. It's not like I won't go back at some point. They even did an overhaul of the security system at the house and the offices downtown. I had to draw the line at letting them hire me a bodyguard. My mother is convinced that Kendal will be coming after me at some point. I don't know why she feels that way; she claims its mother's intuition. Daddy keeps telling her to stop mentioning it because it's actually really starting to freak me out. I know she means well and is worried about me, but seriously? I have a more pressing issue to think about right now.

I crawl up on the top slat of the wooden fence around the training pen and watch Stella run in circles around the large ring. Earlier today, I went to the doctor because I woke up feeling nauseous and gross. It was the second morning in a row. After doing some tests and an ultrasound on my abdomen, my fear of being pregnant was confirmed. Nate and I had made a little nugget of life, which is currently nestled in my uterus. I'm freaking out about it and have yet to tell Nate.

My parents like Nate a lot more as a person now, even though when they first saw us kiss, neither of them was too happy. Really, their dislike only had to do with their irrational fear that being close to him would make me even more of a target for Kendal. After telling them about everything that had been going on since day one, literally as in the day his dad died, they softened and accepted him as the man I was choosing to spend my time with. Outside of the business arena, Nate and my dad had become golfing buddies and friends. He commented to me one night about how much Nate reminded him of Russell. I encouraged him to tell Nate that. I don't know if he ever did.

I miss Shelby so much. I miss her sass, her complaining

about most things, her friendship, and her companionship. Everything. I miss everything about her. While Stella continues to prance around the ring, enjoying her free time, I look beyond the trees and at the house on the rise. After that night, Nate had the house closed up. Everything was packed away in boxes that were stacked in the rooms they previously occupied. Furniture was covered with sheets, and the windows and doors were bolted shut. He even went so far as to add a new high-tech security system to the property, house, and business.

It was a rough time for us both. There were a lot of tears shed, a lot of "what ifs", "maybe if we did it differently", accusations, apologies, and more tears. In the end, we did what we thought was best. Nate took over the daily operations of Bowman Farm while also continuing to run things with his own company. It was time-consuming for sure, but we made it work.

A month after Shelby was taken and her body hadn't surfaced, the police began to slowly back off on the investigation. All of their leads had gone cold. The evidence wasn't giving them anything they didn't already know, and they were getting pressure from the mayor to set the public's fear at ease. They released a press release saying that the killer seemed to have moved on from the area, and there was nothing for anyone to worry about. After that, Nate, my parents, and I decided to have a private empty casket burial for Shelby in my family's plot at the local cemetery. It was our way of saying goodbye without publicly letting go of the woman we all loved so much.

Officer Gaines had contacted me shortly after the press release to let me know that she had convinced the Mayor to leave the case open, some added pressure from my father didn't hurt, and that she would be continuing to work on it and try to find more clues that were maybe missed the first, second, third and even fourth time they had gone over it. I appreciated this more than she could ever know. Losing Shelby was like losing a piece of myself. To all intents and purposes, we were twins. Losing her hurt my soul. Not just then, but even now. My soul aches for her every day.

"Ms Harper?" It's the trainer that Nate hired specifically for Stella once Shelb...

"Yes?"

"John is on the phone in the office for you. He says there's someone here to see you."

"Okay. Do you mind getting Stella back in the stable and giving her a good grooming while I take his call?"

"Not at all."

"Thanks!" I throw the words over my shoulder as I walk through the stable doors and into the trainer's office. The smell of manure and hay briefly makes my stomach roll before it settles once again. Lifting the phone from the receiver, I say, "John? It's Harper. What's up?"

"Hey, Ms Harper. I wanted to let you know that Officer Gaines is on her way up to see you."

Officer Gaines? "Did she mention the reason for her visit?" "NO ma'am she just rolled up and asked if you were here."

"Okay, thanks, John." After hanging up the phone, I head out of the office and to the front of the stable ready to welcome my unexpected guest.

Meanwhile, across town and deep underneath the limestone

143

cliffs at "*the spot*".

"Shelby." Kendal is saying my name in that stupid singsong voice that she uses when she wants to annoy the fuck out of me. Which is every day. "I brought you a friend." *No... please don't let it be...* When she comes into view from around the corner, I rush from my makeshift bed on the hard cold floor to the Plexiglas wall that shows me the entire cavern where Kendal has kept me for weeks to see her pushing a brown-haired woman on a table with wheels.

My relief is palpable when I realize it isn't Harper or Nate, but it is quickly replaced by sadness for the woman about to meet a similar fate as me. Anger that I can't do anything about it, and sickness from the thought of having to see what she will do to another living being. Instead of putting her in the cell next to mine, she moves her limp body onto the table in the middle of her "stage," as she refers to it. The sick thought that she must have gotten bored with only torturing me, that she had to go and steal another person to murder, makes my body heave, and I spew bile all over the window through which I see my future.